S. E. Gilchrist can't remember a time when she didn't have a book in her hand. Now she dreams up stories where her favourite words are ... 'what if' and 'where'? Writing as both S. E. Gilchrist and Suzanne Gilchrist, she loves combining romance with adventure and suspense across many different genres including science fiction/space opera, apocalyptic, and contemporary small towns.

An Australian writer, SE now lives in South East Queensland.

Author's website: www.segilchrist.com

Other Books By the Author

Writing as: SUZANNE GILCHRIST

Cowboy under the Mistletoe (Edge of the Outback Romance)
Dance in the Outback (Edge of the Outback Romance)
The Cowboy's Gift (Edge of the Outback Romance)
Under an Outback Sky (Edge of the Outback Romance)

Love's Sweet Challenge (Bindarra Creek Short & Sweet Romance)
Take Me Home (Bindarra Creek A Town Reborn)
A Dangerous Secret (former title - Amulet of Death) (A Bindarra Creek Mystery Romance)
The Mistletoe Wish (A Bindarra Creek Christmas Romance)
The Glitter or The Gold (Bindarra Creek Small Town Christmas)

Writing as: S. E. GILCHRIST

SCIENCE FICTION/SPACE OPERA ROMANCE

Darkon Warriors series:
Legend Beyond the Stars
The Portal
Awakening the Warriors
Star Pirate's Justice
When Stars Collide
Bargain with the Enemy
Touring the Stars
The Slave Trap

Mars Academy Series:
Stranded

Cosmic Fire

Apocalyptic/Dystopian*:*
Paying the Forfeit
Storm of Fire
Don't Look Back (Warders of Earth)
Quest for Earth

CONTEMPORARY
Bindarra Creek Makeover (Bindarra Creek Romance)
Endangered Heart (Hero
Scent of the Jaguar (Deadly Forces series)
Cotton Field Dreams (Mindalby Outback Romance)

FANTASY/ANCIENT WORLDS EROTIC ROMANCE
Bound by Love
Bound by Lies

The Glitter or The Gold

(Bindarra Creek Small Town Christmas)

By

Suzanne Gilchrist

For my daughter for her courage.
From the first moment I saw you, you captured my heart.

Chapter One

Humming along to the catchy song on the radio, Billie Miller scrubbed the area around the tiny hole in the car's exhaust pipe with a steel toothed brush. Once satisfied she'd eliminated the dirt and rust, she smoothed it off with a fine grit sandpaper. Tossing the sandpaper to one side, she took a moment to wipe beads of sweat from her forehead with the sleeve of her overalls. Although it was only late September, the tin shed she was working in thrummed with stifling heat. If this was a sign of the weather to come, she'd be wise to organise a swimming pool membership. Either that or spend the summer floating in the rock pool in Ward's Gully.

Which didn't sound like such a bad idea now that she came to think about it. Pausing, she imagined a picnic beneath shady willow trees with her elderly parents. A perfect memory to treasure; and a blessing if she could pull it off because the truth was, she didn't possess many happy family day memories. Not recent ones anyway; and that fault lay entirely on her shoulders and her obsession with building a successful mechanic business far from the small town of Bindarra Creek.

But that life was over, and here she was in her hometown living with her parents again at the ripe old age of thirty-nine - and counting.

She twitched her shoulders to push aside her unpleasant thoughts. Best not revisit the past or she'd never finish the job on hand. With a wiggle of her butt, she shifted the dolly-trolley she lay on under the old station wagon a tad to the right then groped for the bottle of acetone and a clean rag.

The song ended and immediately another Christmas tune took its place. The local station was seriously into the Christmas spirit even though there was still plenty of time before the holiday season began.

What would Christmas look like this year? Would her father even realise it *was* Christmas? Anguish gripped and twisted hard. Dementia was a real kick in the teeth for someone who had spent his entire life administering and helping others. *Life could be cruel.* But she had only herself to blame for staying away so long. At least, her father still recognised her. That was a blessing for which she was grateful for every day.

Flicking on her torch, she played the beam over the

problem area. The small crack looked ready for the next step – applying the wet exhaust tape around the pipe. About to reach for the tape she paused as footsteps sounded over the hard concrete floor.

"Hello? Is anyone here?" called a pleasant male voice.

Her breathing hitched. She recognised that voice. Glaring at the undercarriage of the car, she willed her suddenly racing pulse to steady. That soft Yankee drawl had to belong to Kirk Wellington, given he was the only American in town. He'd arrived about four months ago, not that long after she had returned home. Apparently, he was an actor of all things and a relative of Ms Edwina Lette and her grandson, Dodge. Which unfortunately for Billie, meant too many encounters with him as her own mother and Ms Lette had always been tight as if an invisible bungee cord bound them together. Hence Billie had called her Auntie Edwina since she could talk. Even so, Billie had done her best to avoid him as much as possible on the occasions when she'd found herself in his company. He oozed sex appeal but it was more his engaging friendliness that disturbed her the most, triggering her hard-won defence system. She didn't need another relationship complication in her life – ever.

Which was a pity because he had the most tantalising smile and a way of holding her gaze as if she was someone truly special. With her hands motionless in the air, she stared blankly at the chassis above while she wasted a pleasant three whole seconds thinking about that smile until the sound of a throat clearing snapped her back to reality.

Annoyed with herself, she propelled out from under the car like a rocket, pushed to her feet and directed her scowl at the man who had recently begun to appear in her dreams. Not that she intended to admit it to anyone.

"Well?"

"Hi, there." His sparkling hazel eyes travelled over her dusty figure and his smile broadened into a grin. "I thought you might like to share lunch with me. Since it's my car you're working on."

"You're paying me. Or rather paying the garage owner," Billie said with a haughty sniff tacked on for good measure. "And no thanks, I'm not hungry."

Her stomach gave a traitorous growl.

Raising his eyebrows, Kirk waggled a large brown paper bag with grease stains in front of her face, giving her a good whiff of something seriously tasty. Was that a rissole and gravy sanga?

Her mouth watered.

"Courtesy of Warren's fabulous cooking. Do you know him?"

Billie shoved her hands into her pockets so she wouldn't be tempted to snatch the bag and wolf down the contents. "Of course, I do. He's Auntie's son-in-law or rather he was – before his first wife passed away."

"Mom told me how Cheryl died – snake bite – at Christmas time, if I remember correctly. That must have been devastating for everyone."

"Yeah, it was awful. I was maybe fifteen or sixteen at the time, and poor Dodge had just finished primary school. A terribly young age to lose your mother."

"Did you know her well?"

"Not so much. I only saw her at the shops or when I visited Auntie Edwina's place. I guess I was a typical teenager, self-absorbed back then; but I remember the funeral. Almost the entire town turned out to pay their respects. I remember thinking how shattered Warren and Auntie Edwina looked. Poor Dodge looked bewildered, as if he was stuck in some terrible dream."

"Or nightmare."

"Yeah." She looked away for a few beats, thinking back, about how the community, especially her parents, had rallied behind the bereaved family. About how kind people could be when needed. Feeling sad and a little guilty over how much she'd forgotten about her early life growing up in Bindarra Creek.

"Mom and dad left us kids with a nanny and flew over for a couple of days to give any support they could. Sad times, indeed. I can't image how Dylan must have felt. We're the same age, you know," said Kirk.

Lifting her chin, Billie gave him a tiny smile, trying to shift the sombre spell cast by past shadows. "Dodge, remember? Only Mrs Brown calls him Dylan. Not even his own dad."

"They seem close."

"They are that. Warren's a good bloke. He deserves to

be happy and according to Mum, he is now thanks to Lou and the twins."

Kirk gave a theatrical shudder. "Those boys! Talk about energy! And the noise they make when they're chasing the dog around the house. Makes me exhausted listening to them." He grinned to show there was no malice behind his words. "Now, getting back to Warren and his divine cooking. I all but gallop down the stairs these days for breakfast and dinner. Which is playing havoc with my weight."

With a dramatic sigh, he patted his flat stomach. The faded blue jeans he wore hugged slim hips, firm thighs and long legs that ended above a pair of neon-green Nikes.

Billie's stare zeroed in on what was no doubt a six-pack stomach that rippled with muscles, hating the quivering deep in her belly. No sign of any excess weight that she could see. Had he done that on purpose? Directed her eyes to his body? Could he be teasing her? She already knew he liked to flirt. From what she'd seen, he seemed to direct his charm impartially onto anyone and everyone. She knew better than to believe he was seriously attracted to her especially since she was older than him by a few years. Now, if she was a young twenty-something year old, then matters might well be different. Not that *she* was interested of course.

"The food is getting cold." He opened the bag, releasing more of that aromatic scent.

Freshly baked bread. Rissoles. Gravy. Who could resist?

"I guess I could stop for a few minutes." Billie moved past and pumped the de-greaser bottle. After drying off on a clean rag she marched towards the open roller door. "Shall we eat outside? The garage's new owners have erected a shade awning with a table and chair arrangement out the back."

"Already spotted it. I've got a small cooler there with cold water and a couple of cans of soda."

"I could have said no."

"Ah, but I've experienced first-hand the power of these meatballs."

Billie couldn't help it; she laughed as she walked out into the warm sunny day and made her way to the rear of the building. Her neck prickled as Kirk strolled behind her, seemingly making no effort to catch up and walk by her side. If he was inspecting her backside, then good luck to him. The overalls she wore covering her tank top and shorts were so baggy they could have fit an elephant. Definitely very unfeminine.

She swung around to glare at him, only to be caught up short. Instead of admiring her, he was staring at the mural painted on the side of the garage wall.

"Impressive." He waved a hand to encompass the vibrant image of the Akuna River raging through the gorge in the national park and a red-tailed black cockatoo soaring high in the blue arc of sky. "How come I didn't notice this painting before?"

"Because this side of the wall is only visible to people approaching the town from the south. The painting is a big tourist attraction ever since the town's progress association pushed hard for the building to be included in the Silo – Water Tank Art Trail even though it's on a garage wall."

"It sure is something."

Together they reached the small square of concrete where a plastic table and four chairs had been set up.

Slipping onto one of the chairs, she retrieved the bottles of water, placing them on the table. "Thanks for this, looks like you've thought of everything."

"Could do with some dill pickles. You Aussies don't seem to be big on any kind of pickles," mourned Kirk as he settled onto the hard plastic chair opposite her. He offered her the bag first. A display of manners that she wished didn't impress but did.

As if he'd sensed he'd scored a point in his favour, he winked and took a drink of cold water before saying, "Since I brought gifts, how about a discount?"

Billie breathed in the delicious meaty smell and smiled. "Not my call, mate. You need to talk to the boss."

Kirk chatted on while she made short work of her sandwich. "I was hoping for a good word from you. Never mind. I didn't pay much for the old gal anyway, so I can't complain. Stroke of luck that I was able to find a car so easily that was in my budget."

"You were probably ripped off. How much did the wagon cost?"

When he told her, she swallowed a large mouthful then grinned. "That was way too much for that old rust bucket. I bet you got it from Roy Towns. He's known in Bindarra Creek as a bit of a collector. He scours the countryside, buys all sorts of cheap stuff, and tries to up-sell. His yard is full of junk he hasn't managed to get rid of. By the way, your car is full of rust and won't pass the next rego."

A tiny crease appeared between his thin dark brows as he appeared to ponder her words. Immediately an image of him looking grave in a white surgeon's coat sprung to mind. Billie could have kicked herself for remembering. She never should have researched that US daytime soap he'd starred in. Simple curiosity. That was all. Didn't mean a thing.

Kirk took a bite, and finished chewing before asking, "The registration is due a few days before Christmas. How much work is needed?"

"Everything mate. Your tyres are almost bald, there's rust throughout the chassis, the bonnet, the boot and the doors. The car needs a new clutch; the brakes are shot, and the engine made a terrible whine when I turned it over."

"You make it sound like it's at death's door!"

"It's a dud. Cost more than it's worth to repair."

"But he seemed such a nice guy."

Billie finished off her sandwich, noting that he had only eaten half of his. She'd always been a fast eater; her mother used to tell her all the time to slow down, or she'd get a belly ache. But she'd always been in a hurry; a hurry to rush outside to play, a hurry to get to school, finish her homework, watch TV – a hurry to leave this small town behind her. She wiped rissole grease and gravy off her lips with a paper napkin Kirk had provided. Her heart softened a trifle at his pensive expression. "We all get suckered in some time or another. And Mr Towns, although he's a real sweetie at heart, loves when he manages to sell something for a profit. Think of it as your good deed for the year. Besides, you're hardly likely to need a car for much longer. Aren't you only here on holiday? You must be due to go back to the States soon."

"Hmmm. It's possible my stay may be extended." Kirk gazed off into the distance. His face relaxed, his lips curving into a slow sexy smile as if he entertained very pleasant thoughts.

What the devil was he thinking?

And *who* was he thinking of?

And, anyway, didn't he have a star-studded, glittering career to return to? She couldn't imagine Hollywood waiting for anyone. Even someone as charismatic as Kirk. If he didn't want to become a has-been, then he had better hightail it back to the States.

Her cheeks heated and ducking her head, Billie busied herself with scrunching up the paper bag, fiddling with the water bottles, anything so she wouldn't catch his far too discerning eyes. "Well, that's lunch done. I better get back to it."

Turning, Kirk pinned her in place with his intense gaze. "Do you enjoy being a mechanic?"

"What can I say? I love engines. Love the smell of grease and oil. I would spend all day tinkering under the hood if I could. I used to buy damaged bicycles and repair them just for fun. Fixing stuff is my jam." Billie shrugged as if trying to make light of the passion that sang strongly in her words.

"I admire anyone who can fix things. I'm a bit hopeless in that regard."

"We all have our strengths," Billie mumbled and made to stand.

Kirk reached over and placed a hand on her arm. His touch was light, tentative almost, but it had the potency to freeze her in place. "I had more than one reason behind my gift of food."

"Oh?" Her pulse thundered in her ears as she stared at his hand, her brain dissolving into mush. Should she flick it off? Tell him to never touch her again? His skin was warm and yet somehow scorched through the overalls to her very bone. She had to get back to work; apart from the exhaust on his car, she had another two minor services to complete before the day's end. And yet she didn't move.

His hand slid off her arm to rest on the table.

Billie slumped into her chair, feeling as if she'd just done a round with her father's favourite boxer. "What reason?" Was he going to ask her on a date? What would she say? She'd sworn off relationships – for good. And this guy with his easy charm and friendly manner reminded her far too much of her ex for her peace of mind.

Although...maybe a dinner out with a good-looking guy was just what she needed to reassure herself she was still attractive. That *she* could be valued above all else.

"I need a favour." His smile was guileless as he gazed earnestly at her.

Not a date then.

What had she been thinking? Early in the new year, she would hit forty. Although she kept in reasonably good shape thanks to her fondness for swimming and surfing, she'd never had much interest in maintaining any sort of beauty regime. Her skin was now paying the price for all those years spent in the ocean. And her hair – let's not mention her coarse blonde hair.

Wake up Billie. Not a date.

A favour.

Her stupid daydream of a dinner together vaporised while the faint taste of rissoles and gravy turned to ash in her mouth. "I don't do favours." Her voice came out harsh.

He looked a little surprised at her tone. "That's a shame. Still, I'll ask anyway as it's for a good cause. I'm organising a play, for Christmas, and I need someone to help with the set. You said yourself you enjoy fixing things."

No date.

No desire to spend one-on-one time in her company.

No attraction on his part.

Which meant that electricity zinging between them was a figment of her lonely imagination.

"The proceeds from ticket sales will be donated to a charity for homeless women and children," he cajoled and gave her one of his mega-watt smiles.

Billie surged to her feet and began to briskly pack away the esky. Who could say no to such a worthwhile cause? "Sure. Why not."

It shouldn't be too hard. All she had to do was bash out a couple of sets, maybe do a bit of painting and job done. All for a good cause.

And no dinner date in sight.

Which suited her perfectly. Or did it?

Chapter Two

Kirk strolled along the road that led back to Fig Tree Lodge, the house jointly owned by his mother, her two sisters Elspeth and Janice and her cousin Edwina Lette, whistling, and feeling pretty darned pleased with himself. His visit had gone better than anticipated. He felt like rubbing his hands together with glee, like a small child who'd won the biggest and the best prize in the school. But that wouldn't do. Billie wasn't a prize, or a trophy. She was a strong, beautiful woman who touched him on so many levels he wouldn't know where to start if he had to list them all.

Meeting Billie had sure turned his entire future upside down and inside out, overshadowing the lure of fame and fortune. It looked as if having his own star embedded in the Hollywood Walk of Fame had been well and truly trounced by a certain prickly and elusive blonde. Who would have thought he'd travel halfway across the world to meet the only woman he'd ever entertained spending his life with? All he had to do, was convince her he was the man for her. But what had previously seemed so easy with other women was proving to be a lot harder than he'd ever imagined. His famous charm had, so far, gotten him nowhere. Billie Miller acted as if she was determined to remain single with her heart well and truly unattached. After a lot of rumination, he'd concluded he had to play to his strengths and that was when the idea of a Christmas play had materialised.

And that was a whole other challenge!

His phone buzzed signalling a message had come through. Kirk didn't bother to check. He knew without looking it would be another text from his agent demanding to know when he'd be stateside again. Not that that mattered, given any decent offers for new roles appeared to have dried up lately. A bit like the drought that had hit his home state of California in recent months.

In the distance came the faint mooing of cows. And just that morning while he'd been sipping his first coffee on the porch, there had even been a kangaroo grazing on the front lawn of Fig Tree Lodge. Imagine that! A real-life kangaroo in your yard.

He stared around eagerly but saw no further sign of

those cute weird-looking animals. Probably dozing out of the blazing sun, if they had any sense. Heat pulsed from the concrete beneath his feet, the phone in his pocket bumping against his body with each step he took, reminding him of the life he'd left behind. Even if he was offered the role of a lifetime, he hadn't made up his mind about when that would be. The thought of leaving this small place on Earth troubled him. The original idea had been to accompany his mother and his sister to visit relatives he'd barely known existed let alone met before. They'd stay a few months re-connecting, doing some sight-seeing before heading home. Somehow the days had turned into weeks, and then suddenly four months had passed and neither he nor his family had made a move to book their return tickets.

A trickle of sweat inched down his forehead and dripped into his eye causing it to sting and water. He stopped in the middle of the cracked sidewalk, dropped the cooler he carried on the ground then removed his shades and rubbed. Behind him came the shrill trill of a bicycle bell. Blinking, he turned then had to snatch up the cooler and hurriedly leap to the side as a tandem bicycle veered towards him.

He waved, a grin stretching across his face as he recognised the elderly couple lurching to a halt a few feet away. Billie's parents.

"Kirk! How lovely to see you. Jonas and I are having our daily constitutional. Are you heading back to Edwina's?" A flushed Mrs Florrie Miller patted the bike's basket where several items bulged beneath a checked cloth. "We're calling in with some scones and thought we'd have a cuppa with her and your mother."

Even though he'd just finished lunch, Kirk's mouth watered. He'd always been a sucker for homemade scones. However, he'd pass on the tea idea. It was just plain weird how Aussies loved consuming bucketloads of the stuff on even the hottest of days. Give him a bottle of cold spring water any day. "Sounds great. I've been to see Billie."

Mrs Miller nodded while her husband who had a serene face that made him look younger than his years belying the tufts of white hair poking out from under his helmet, gave a start and said, "Huh? Billie? We've got a daughter called Billie."

"Yes, that's right. I just spoke to her a few minutes ago," Kirk said in a calm tone. "How are you today, Mr Miller?"

"Who's this? Who's this man?" Jonas pointed a shaking finger in his direction.

"This is Kirk, Edwina's cousin's son from California, Jonas, love. He's over here on holidays."

A vague expression replaced the momentary alertness, the old man dropping his gaze as he picked at a sore on the back of his hand.

Florrie Miller's thin nose quivered as she frowned at Kirk, scanning his red face. "You need to get yourself a proper hat. Not one of those baseball caps either. Something with a decent brim."

"I bought one online the other day. It should arrive soon." Kirk fingered his own nose which did feel decidedly hot to the touch.

"Excellent. Until then, plenty of sunscreen," Mrs Miller made to mount the bike again. "We'll be on our way, then. Come on, Jonas. We've got scones and jam waiting to be eaten."

"I like scones." Jonas smiled at Kirk.

Kirk smiled back. "So do I."

"Please join us. We've made plenty." Mrs Miller gave a nod of thanks when he stepped onto the road to give the older couple plenty of room. The bike wobbled off and Kirk had to admire their fortitude given the sun seared down from a cloudless sky with a savage ferocity guaranteed to cook anything in its path.

He hoisted the cooler once more and, picking up his pace, followed.

When he reached the shady grounds of Fig Tree Lodge, he made his way to the back of the house, entering through the kitchen door to find the room empty. The sound of voices uplifted in laughter and cheerful arguments drew him into the formal living room.

His cousin, no that wasn't right, his first cousin once removed, Edwina Lette, sat like an elderly queen presiding over her court on an intricately carved armchair while family and friends clustered about on less imposing chairs. With her small, thin physique and lined, drawn features she should have been dwarfed by the large piece of furniture, and yet, somehow, she seemed to own the space. She had a presence that couldn't be denied and one that Kirk admired immensely. If he had only half her magnetism, his success in Hollywood could have no limits.

The second he stepped into the room, she looked over, keen hazel eyes punching into his like laser beams. Her smile had a mischievous quality that energised his curiosity while warning him to tread carefully. He'd learned the hard way to be wary of that particular look.

"We were just talking about you, Kirk. Pull up a chair and help yourself to a scone." She waved a wrinkled hand, like a royal demand, in the direction of a tea trolley crammed with plates, cups and a teapot.

Mentally making a note to run an extra four miles later that day, he grabbed a plate, loaded it with two still-warm scones, buttered then piled on a dollop of black-berry jam, topping it all off with clotted cream. Juggling his plate, he poured out a cup of thick, black tea and perched on the edge of the settee next to his sister, Pixie. Dipping his chin, he grinned. "Got food on your face, sis."

"Oh, thanks. It's just that the jam is so delish, I've eaten three scones already." Rubbing at the offending stain around her mouth, Pixie stared mournfully at the crumbs on her plate.

Still feeling those gimlet eyes drilling into him, Kirk turned to Edwina with an easy smile. "Should I be worried?"

Raising her hands, Edwina stared down into her open palms. "Only if you don't take up the challenge and embrace your fate," she said, a sly smirk spreading over her wrinkled face.

An equally elderly woman, ramrod straight as any soldier, perched on the edge of a hard-backed chair as if about to spring into action at any second, snorted. "I wish you wouldn't practice your mumbo-jumbo all the time, Edwina. It's very irritating." Mrs Pamela Brown, widow, and who Kirk understood was one of Edwina's oldest, and probably closest, friend. And probably the only one who could get away with admonishing her.

Edwina assumed an expression of holier-than-thou and replied in a lofty tone, "I can't help if I have the gift."

"What piffle. Utter nonsense," barked Mrs Brown.

Pixie giggled behind her hand while Kirk's mother cast the combating ladies an uneasy glance. Kirk enjoyed his first scone and took note of the other people in the room, nodding as he recognised the faces. There were Billie's parents, Mrs Brown and her shy younger sister, Mrs Fukuka and Makishi, her Japanese husband, his own mother and sister of course, then Mrs Ainsley, looking cool in a pastel green dress and who still projected the persona of a librarian with her black-rimmed glasses despite being retired for many years. He exchanged smiles with Hazel Williams, her hands gnarled and knotted from crippling arthritis, sitting quietly in her wheelchair and her husband, Frank with his bushy grey beard, next to her. Then there were the dogs, the ancient looking poodle, Rajah, and young Boris, the dachshund, sniffing for crumbs on the floor. A small gathering for once but not unexpected since it was a weekday. Dylan, that is, Dodge, and his wife Tessa would be at their shop, their kids in school. Warren and Lou were absent, no doubt in their own home which used to be an old stable block on the same property and had been converted into separate living quarters. Their twins, thank heavens, also in school. The middle-aged couple who had arrived yesterday as guests of the Lodge were no doubt busy visiting local tourist spots.

Florence Miller pressed another scone onto her husband who sat relaxed beside her and said as if the other two women hadn't spoken. "Tell us about the play, please, Kirk. Everyone can't wait to hear more."

Her placid voice and the way she steered the conversation into less dangerous waters, told Kirk she had had plenty of practice over the years. Not only due to her long association with her friends but also due to her roles in the community; first as a vicar's wife and now as the vicar, after her husband had stepped down due to ill-health. Kirk had been impressed with her sermons and the aura of peace she seemed to imbibe the services each Sunday. He'd never been a regular church goer back home; but with Edwina expecting everyone in the household to attend every week in support of her old friend, he'd somehow found himself tagging along and enjoying the experience.

"I'm calling it, the Mystery of the Missing Pudding."

He paused to eat more of his scone; and also, to imbibe a sense of drama.

"Well, get on with it. Don't keep us in suspense," demanded Edwina, snatching up a chocolate from a dish on the coffee table, stuffing it into her mouth while her friend, Pamela clicked her tongue in dismay. Kirk understood she had had a few health scares recently and was supposed to be following a strict diet; a restriction she didn't often follow, and which often led to a few arguments around the dinner table.

"It's a script I've been working on the past couple of years. A comedic murder mystery whodunit set in the 1920's."

"Like an Agatha Christie only humorous?" queried Hazel Williams, leaning forward, and looking interested.

"Exactly." Kirk beamed, his chest swelling proudly as he considered his story which was his first foray into the writing genre. "There's a few minor plot points I need to flesh out but the characters and the overall mystery arc are complete. I thought the proceeds from ticket sales could go to a charity that supports homeless women and children."

"Well done," declared Mrs Miller. She produced a tattered notebook and a pen from her handbag. "You'll need help. Let's make a list. Now, about the venue."

Kirk took a sip of scalding hot tea and swallowed hurriedly. "Is there a hall nearby that isn't too costly?"

"The C W A hall. Country Women's Association," Edwina clarified for Kirk and his family's benefit. "We won't charge you a hiring fee since it's for a good cause."

Mrs Brown boomed in her firm voice, "The old cinema might be a better idea, Edwina. It has a larger platform stage with exits on both sides that lead to a long room running behind the stage. That area could be sectioned off with dividers for changing costumes and so forth."

"That does sound perfect. I thought Dodge and Tessa may have period furniture that could be used for the set. And I've asked Billie for help building the back drops for each scene." Heat rose over his cheeks as he mentioned her name.

"I'd like to be involved," Pixie piped up. "And Mom, too."

His mother, Louisa, started, her eyes going wide as everyone turned to look at her. "Well, I was thinking we should be going home soon."

"Rubbish. You've only just arrived. We have too many years to make up for. You can't go running off until at least after Christmas. I have plans." Edwina gave a wicked smile.

"If you're sure we won't be a bother."

"Always welcome and I've already told Tessa not to book out your rooms for the duration. Fig Tree Lodge belongs to you, too. Although it's really more my home than yours." It was obvious Edwina was keen to make that point very clear since she'd mentioned it several times in his mother's hearing.

"Then I'd love to accept your invitation, although..." Louisa hesitated for a moment. "If we are staying for Christmas, would you mind if my husband comes over? And also is there a vacant room to accommodate Orlando if he's keen to have a brief holiday here?"

"Of course. It won't be a problem. It will be great to see Norris again and meet your other son. Now, the play." Edwina swept her eagle gaze around the room and Kirk gained the sense that everyone snapped to attention. "We'll make up posters asking for people to try out for character roles, and for volunteers behind the scenes, which I'm certain won't be a problem. Let's also get the request out on our community's Facebook noticeboard, too. Pam and Beatrix can organise costumes with Esther's assistance. Her knowledge of history is exceptional."

The three elderly women nodded, Esther flushing with pleasure at the praise.

Frank Williams exchanged one of those long-married couple's looks with Hazel, clearing his throat. "The back areas of the cinema haven't been used in a long time. I can give it a good clean, once we've got approval to use it. I'm worried there could be vermin."

Hazel held up a shaky hand. "I'd like to take on the advance ticket sales, if that's okay?"

"The job's yours. Now, Pixie, you can design the posters. We'll need those as soon as possible. We'll need to brainstorm some ways to raise funds to get the play off the ground. There will be incidental expenses, even with volunteers. Tessa's the person who can help there. She can also update our community noticeboard, too. I'll find out when the cinema will be available." Edwina clapped her hands together, a broad grin on her face. "Kirk, how many dates were you thinking for the play to run?"

"Just the one night. Perhaps a few weeks before Christmas?" he proposed, gazing around the room. Mrs Miller was scribbling like mad in her notebook while Mrs Brown and Mr and Mrs Williams added more suggestions in low voices. Everyone's faces glowed with eagerness to get started.

"Who knows, if it's a success this could be the beginning of a new annual event." Edwina sat back in her chair, her face softening with approval as she nodded at him. "You've accepted the challenge then. You won't be sorry."

Not knowing what she was talking about and a little dazed at how fast his vague idea was materialising into fact, Kirk felt his chest tighten. "Thanks everyone. I appreciate it."

Chapter Three

The small town of Bindarra Creek buzzed with anticipation. Billie could feel the emotion crackling around her as she made her way along Main Street where the townsfolk either browsed amongst the *'first Tuesday of the month'* market stalls lining both sides of the road or ambled about doing their weekly shopping. From snippets of the conversations, she overheard as she passed by knots of people, she realised the hot topic of the day - was the forthcoming Christmas play.

And the attractive American actor organising it.

Stopping outside the IGA store, she stood on tiptoe to see over a bunch of people's heads crowded around the noticeboard.

A pack of giggling teenagers tore themselves away

and Billie found herself facing the poster announcing *'The Mystery of the Missing Pudding'*; a title that made her smile. It seemed that Kirk had wasted no time in forging ahead with his plans, she admired that in a man. The opposite of *'he-who-shall-not-be-named'*.

Her gaze travelled down the poster, her mind absorbing the details. The date had been pinned down to Saturday, the ninth of December.

The venue – the old cinema.

Ticket prices were displayed along with details of who to contact to purchase advance seats of choice at a slightly higher price.

The name of the charity that would benefit was high-lighted in bold letters, together with a short blurb detailing the work they did along with the demographics that would benefit.

The call to arms for volunteers and actors was prom-inent and a fun time was promised to all.

Billie gave a little shake of her head as she recognised all the names listed as to who to contact for what. There was no question whatsoever that her mother and her cronies were the power behind the man. Maybe he wasn't that proactive after all! Although she knew from experi-ence that once the C W A ladies were involved, they would take over like a well-organised machine. She was certain that should they decide to launch a rocket into space they would succeed. Nothing could beat good old-fashioned common sense, in her opinion.

As she moved out of the way to allow others to read

the announcement, Billie acknowledged the tingle of excitement surging through her veins. What was even more surprising was the sharp disappointment she felt at the lack of contact from Kirk since he'd roped her into this event. She'd expected him to use the opportunity to badger and bombard her with texts. However, she'd heard nothing from him, apart from a single message telling her that he'd be in touch soon.

His idea of soon was nothing like hers.

Since he'd broached his idea that day at the garage, her mind had been teaming with thoughts about the story, who the characters were, who the players would be, what was required from her, and when would she begin. The lack of any further dialogue had infused a curiosity that ate at her, like a starving mouse nibbling away at a block of cheese. Hungry. Insatiable. Impatient.

She was antsy, anxious to get started, and she may as well admit it, overflowing with downright nosiness about what was going on.

And let's not mention how deep down inside, that need to set eyes on him once more grew stronger each passing day.

Twelve whole days.

She refused to admit how many hours and minutes. She wasn't a star-struck teenager for heaven's sake! About to dart inside the IGA for milk and bread she paused when someone called out her name. Turning, she spied Tessa Myers manning a stall on the opposite side of the road and waving in her direction, so she changed her mind and headed over.

Tessa started talking the moment Billie came into hearing distance, her dark brown eyes glowing with excitement. "Can you believe the crowd? I can't remember when market days have been this busy. It's fantastic. Mrs Brown and Mrs Fukuka are making a killing with their homemade blackberry wine. If you want to buy a bottle, I suggest you get in quick. My fav is the one with added cinnamon and hazelnut. It's seriously yummy and non-alcoholic too." She nodded towards the stall beside her where the elderly ladies were chatting to prospective customers about the merits of organic home-made verses mass produced products.

Hardly breaking stride, the two women sent beaming smiles at Billie while continuing their conversation.

Tessa asked, "How do you like working for the new owners at the garage?"

"Good. I was very lucky they were able to offer me a job. I like how the work is on a casual basis only. This gives me more time to spend with my parents, as well as a bit of cash to get me by each week."

"That's great." Tessa leaned forward a tad, giving Billie a gentle tap on the back of her hand. "I'm so sorry about Pastor Miller. He's such a sweet man. Let me know if you ever need someone you'd like to talk to – although you've probably got heaps of friends."

"Not really. It seems my so-called friends melted away with my money, and my former school mates are either living elsewhere or we've grown too far apart." Billie drew a sharp breath and met the younger woman's steady gaze. "I'd like to forge new friendships."

"Same. Text me next time you're free and we'll organise a coffee date." Tessa looked over her crowded table, then uttered a sigh. "I wish I could move more of this bric-a-brac. Every time Dodge goes to one of those deceased estate sales, he comes back with more of this stuff. But unfortunately, those type of sales are usually a job lot, take it all kind of thing. Which means we end up with more china and weird ornaments than we'd like. I can't interest you in anything, can I?" She gave Billie a hopeful glance.

Wanting to help her out, Billie examined the goods, her gaze alighting on a puffy-looking hat and grinned. "I couldn't imagine anyone wearing a beanie like that."

"This?" Tessa picked up the object and began to giggle. "It's a tea-pot warmer. I would have given anything to see you put it on your head."

Face burning, Billie opened her mouth, met Tessa's amused eyes then burst into laughter. "What an idiot I am. I should have recognised it. Mum has something similar in the back of her kitchen cupboard, but I can't remember the last time she used it."

"An old-fashioned idea but they do the job." Tessa placed the teapot warmer back onto the table.

Billie ran a finger over the curved outline of the teapot, admiring the tiny pink roses, pale blue forget-me-nots and the green leaves on a crackle effect background.

A delicate gold banding ran along the rims and handle. "This is a lovely-shaped teapot though. And the chintz pattern is gorgeous. It looks expensive." She turned it over to see if the maker had left his mark. Sure enough, there was a slightly faded stamp and date on the bottom. "Royal Albert, 1945. But you've only got fifty dollars marked on it!"

"I know. It's a steal, however, see here? There's numerous cracks running right through the entire lid. One wrong move, and it will shatter. Such a pity because it's a beautiful piece, plus there's a matching sugar bowl and creamer that goes with it, although the sugar bowl doesn't have a lid. Must have been lost somewhere in time." Tessa tilted her head to one side, tossing back her long brown hair. "Interested?"

"I am, as I'm certain I can fix it so the cracks will be hardly noticeable. The set will make a great Christmas gift for Mum. The teapot she has now is about a zillion years old. And she doesn't have an actual sugar bowl or creamer. I'm certain Mum won't care there isn't a lid for the sugar bowl. I'll take it." Billie dug in the fabric cross-over handbag she wore for her wallet.

"Great choice." Tessa winked. "And the cozy?"

Billie smiled. "Sure. Why not."

"Excellent." Tessa began to wrap the china carefully in sheets of newspaper. "Do you need a bag? I have a few string or fabric totes I could sell you? I try to use as little plastic as possible, so I have none of those. Or I could pop the set into a cardboard box?"

"Box please. Plus, I *will* have one of those fabric totes. The one with the turtle pattern. Thanks."

Tessa placed the wrapped china inside a cardboard box, settling the tote on top. After told the amount owing, Billie paid, then rested her hands on the box, looking around at the bustling scene. A four-wheel-drive followed by a dual-cab ute crawled at a snail's pace down the road, no doubt wary of any pedestrians who might suddenly decide to dart across to grab a bargain.

"If you're into Halloween, there's a stall a bit further along with a great display of gothic costumes and hollowed out pumpkins. Also, Penny has a second-hand book stall, just outside her shop. She's got a good display of old records too if you're into that kind of thing." Tessa took a sip of water from her bottle. "I missed you at yoga, last Saturday."

Billie shrugged, turning back to face the younger woman. "I've taken on a new project and wanted to get started."

"Oh yes." Tessa gave a dreamy smile. "You're doing the backdrops for Kirk's play. He's such lovely guy. And single I believe..." Raising thin dark eyebrows, she allowed the suggestion to trail off.

"I'm not in the market," Billie said shortly, hating how her pulse had raced at the mere mention of his name.

"Mmmm. I did hear on the grape vine a little about your past. I'm sorry you had such a hard time. You know what small towns are like – everyone's business is, well, everyone's business. I was used to no one else looking out for me apart from my good friend, Maki. When I first came here, I hated how everyone wanted to poke their nose in. But then I had first-hand experience of the other side of the coin – how this town looks after their own. And of course, here was where I met Dodge, married him, had another daughter, and gained his family as my own."

"You lived in Sydney, didn't you?"

Tessa nodded, a frown knitting her brows. "Yeah, I lived on the streets for a while when I was a teenager. That was tough. I could have so easily slipped into a dangerous life but when my then boyfriend Ian died in a streetcar race I was alone. Not long after, I found out I was pregnant, and I knew I wanted something better for my baby."

"Mum wrote and told me a little about your circumstances. How you went to a kids' refuge where you completed your education. She also mentioned what happened after you and your daughter arrived here in town," Billie said, picking her words with care, not wanting to spell out what must have a horrifying ordeal when a stalker had attempted to kidnap Tessa's daughter.

Tessa grimaced. "Yeah, I thought I'd been clever. But that nasty-piece-of-work is dead now. Someone murdered him in prison, and we don't have to look over our shoulders ever again. Now, enough about me. Are you thinking of staying here permanently?"

"Originally, no. I had thought I would catch up with my parents while I consider my next move."

"And now?"

Billie chewed over the question for a few seconds until Tessa raised her eyebrows and said, "I get it. It's this town. It gets under your skin and kinda wraps itself around you in a way you don't want it to let you go."

Billie laughed. "You've got it in one."

"Personally, it'll be great if you stayed. You can never have too many good friends."

"Thanks."

They exchanged understanding smiles.

Tessa glanced along the street then smiled, her face radiating such a glowing happy expression that Billie wasn't surprised to see her two daughters threading their way through the press of people.

"Hi, Mum," said the eldest, Kaylee, an almost mirror image of her tall mother with the same brown hair and dark eyes. She held the hand of Tilly, her five-year old half-sister who clutched a dog leash at the end of which a happy-looking dachshund strained.

Tilly grinned, revealing a gap where she'd recently lost one of her front baby teeth. "Grannie asked me to buy her a pumpkin. She needs it for her spells." She gave a little skip in a pair of sparkling, crystal studded sandshoes.

Tessa muttered something under her breath that sounded a lot like – 'heaven help us' while Billie attempted to stifle her snigger. She knew all about

'*Grannie*' being how she was her mother's notorious friend, Edwina.

Two giggling teenage girls hemmed in close to Kaylee's other side while behind them were the Taylor boys, so easily distinguishable with their shock of bright red hair, and Noah Davidson. As if knowing exactly what her mother was thinking, Kaylee smirked. "After we check out the Halloween stuff, we're going to help Grannie at her fortune telling stall."

"Ok then, but do *not* do any pretend palm reading. Just help with any sales and keep an eye on Boris." Tessa indicated the little dog. "He's so small, someone might step on him."

"I never thought about that. I'll carry him for a while." Kaylee scooped the wriggling dog into her arms, ignoring the pout that appeared on her sister's face.

"I don't mind holding him for you." Drew Taylor pushed forwards, holding his hands out, an eager expression on his face.

Kaylee passed Boris over and the group of teenagers wandered away.

"You can tell Kaylee is your daughter, you look so alike. And by the way, in case you hadn't noticed, Drew is definitely crushing on her."

"Yeah, I keep telling her she's too young to think about boys, but there are days when she acts as if she's twenty. And others, she's back to being my little girl again. Dodge and I want to hold onto her for as long as we can, but we know her dreams will probably take her far from home."

Billie smiled. "Has she thought about what she might want to do after she leaves school?"

"She has another two years to go which means she could well change her mind. But the latest idea is university to study astronomy." Tessa gave a theatrical shudder as she met Billie's gaze. "To be totally honest, I'll be thankful for anything as long as it doesn't involve palm or tarot reading or communing with ghosts. Both my girls adore Gran, and I don't blame them. She's wonderful and been so kind to me. But the things she gets up to!"

"Don't worry. I know all about Auntie Edwina. I've had to deal with her my entire childhood."

The two women exchanged knowing smiles.

"Grannie certainly keeps all of us on our toes." Tessa straightened, her eyes drifting towards where a middle-aged couple were picking through a pile of old picture frames. "I better see if they are keen to buy something. Lovely to chat, Billie, and if you need any help with the play, let me know. Otherwise, I'll hopefully see you at yoga next Saturday."

Steps brisk with purpose, Billie crossed to the IGA store and entered. Already her mind had leapt ahead to the possibility of a different path than the one she'd been determined to travel since a young girl. What if she stayed in Bindarra Creek? Started a small mechanic business here? Or she could simply continue working at the garage, become her mum's right hand, read to her father, and discuss philosophy with him. Once she became financially secure again, she could purchase a little cottage. She didn't need a McMansion. Something with a yard big enough for a shed where she could work on cars or other machinery. She could purchase an old bicycle, cycle around town, join the local bike-riding group. And after the weekly yoga classes, she could have coffee or brekkie with Tessa and the other members at the Cyprus Café. She could reach out to any former school mates still living in the area. Friendships would be formed. Connections renewed. She could even join the C W A and be on the knitting committee. She could become a productive member of a tight knit community. Maybe even join her mother and her friends each fortnight at the local rifle range.

Her phone buzzed, signalling a text message.

FIRST PLAY MEETING TONIGHT OVER DINNER. 6PM @ RIVERSIDE BISTRO. PLSE REPLY Y OR N – KIRK

About time. Her finger stabbed the 'Y' key and feeling happier than she had in months, Billie checked the list on her mobile and headed to the bakery section. Now all she had to decide on was – what to wear.

Chapter Four

Heart pounding just that little too hard for his comfort, Kirk pulled up outside the vicarage. Flipping down the visor, he checked his reflection, worrying over the lone fleck of grey he spotted in his left eyebrow. Using the tips of his fingers he tugged hard, removing the offending hair. Much better. Uncomfortable with the flutter of nerves causing cold sweat along his spine, he drew a deep breath as he pocketed the keys and swung from the rust bucket of a car he'd bought. A few strides and he was facing the front door. He raised his hand just as it opened, revealing Mrs Miller and her welcoming smile.

"Come in, Kirk." She lowered her voice, beckoning him inside, words flowing from her in a steady stream causing his head to whirl at the deluge of information.

"Jonas is being a trifle difficult with his dinner and Billie has the gift of cajoling him into eating which is such a blessing. Billie will be ready in a jiffy. At our last C W A meeting, Natalie told me Dan's new chef, Carmel, has introduced special menus on some weeknights. Apparently, tonight is 'Spanish' night. Sounds quite exotic although I'm not a fan of spicy food. I do hope that you and Billie will find something edible. Good old-fashioned meat and three vegies is what you get in this house. Now that I've mentioned it, we would love to have you over for dinner one night. Perhaps a day next week?"

While Florrie had been talking, she'd led the way into the eat-in kitchen where her husband and daughter sat at the table.

"I'd love to, thank you." He grinned inwardly as he pretended he hadn't noticed the blush turning Billie's face into a rosy hue. Enchanted he took note of the shine of her blonde hair, and the pale blue dress she wore and how it clung to very enticing curves. She'd gone to some trouble to look her best, and if he squinted just a little bit harder, he was certain there was even makeup on her face. Interesting. "Evening, Mr Miller. How are you?"

The elderly gent's brow wrinkled as he peered with uncertain eyes at Kirk. "Have you come for dinner?"

"No, not tonight. But soon. Your daughter and I are having a meal at the pub instead. I love that shade of blue on you, Billie. How are you this evening?"

Her blush deepened and she peeped at him beneath lowered eyelids. "Good." She turned back to her father who appeared to have a resurgence of his appetite as he demolished the remainder of the food on his plate.

Florrie settled onto a chair and without making a fuss, dished out some kind of pudding into a bowl which she set before her husband before picking up her own spoon. "I'm sure you'll have a lovely time. Natalie also told me there'll be dancing at the pub because someone's having a hen's night and a DJ has been hired."

"We won't be dancing, Mum. It's not a date, we're there to discuss the play."

Unperturbed, Florrie carried on. "Your father and I were quite a hit on the dancefloor in our days. About fifteen years ago, we took up line-dancing wanting to try something new. We came first in the Bindarra Creek Line-Dancing competition one year. Put Edwina's nose out of joint, she was quite certain that she would win again." She chuckled.

Jonas joined in her laughter, either wanting to share in his wife's pleasure or perhaps that golden moment had appeared through the misty curtains of his memories. Kirk sure hoped so. The old guy deserved to hold onto those precious moments for as long as possible. He grinned, imagining a dancefloor filled with grey-haired old biddies tapping their cowboy boots in tune to the classic 'Nutbush' song. Fifteen years ago, his cousin Edwina would have been in her early sixties, while the Millers would have had to have been well into their fifties. The enthusiasm that generation brought to what-ever they tried their hands to, always awed him.

"I think we're finished here. See you later, Dad." Billie bussed her father on the cheek, gave her mother a smile and led the way out of the house.

As he settled behind the steering wheel, Kirk snuck a quick glance at Billie. "Hope you don't mind but I've got someone else to pick up, too."

Delighted at the frown that flittered across her face, he set the car into motion. A high-pitched squeal emitted from the engine for a few seconds before it eased into a stuttering drone.

"Of course not. The more the merrier." Her tone was sour. "How's the car?"

"The old gal has still got some life in her." Kirk patted the dash.

"I doubt it." She turned away to face the side window as they drove down the quiet streets.

It only took a couple of minutes and he pulled up in front of an old, red-brick set of four flats. "I'll only be a moment." Then he was out the door, walking briskly along the cracked concrete drive until he found the middle unit where he rapped on the door.

The young woman must have been watching for him, because she opened it immediately and all but fell out to lay a hand on his arm. He was in two minds about whether that was a good thing if Billie had seen the instant proprietorial move on her part. Giving a nod and a smile, he hustled her towards the car, then rushed around to the driver's seat. "Billie, this is Stacey Richmond. She's in the play. I don't know if you two know each other. Stacey, this is Billie Miller."

"Nah, I don't usually hang with the oldies." Stacey tossed back a flowing mane of hair so gold, Kirk doubted it was genuine. "You're doing the backdrops, aren't you? Funny, I kinda thought you were a bloke."

Billie turned around as Kirk started the car again and smiled at the younger woman. "Easy mistake. I'm named after my paternal grandfather. Nice to meet you, Stacey."

"Yeah, I guess. I didn't know this was going to be a party, Kirk." Disappointment and accusation rang clear in her voice as she shifted forward, all but breathing down his neck.

Kirk edged a little to the side, noticing how Billie was looking at him, amusement written clearly in her face. "Time's not on our side. We must winkle out any inconsistencies in the script now before we start memorising our lines. Stacey's the leading lady," he added for Billie's clarification.

"And Kirk's my leading man," Stacey all but purred in his ear.

Billie made a choked off sound that Kirk wasn't certain was laughter or annoyance. The tension inside the car thickened and he could have sung for joy when the hotel's carpark appeared in his windscreen. It didn't help matters when Stacey slung her arm through his as they all walked into the bistro, Billie tagging along behind. He almost cricked his neck as he twisted around to smile at her inscrutable face, wondering what the devil she was thinking. All the while Stacey kept up a non-stop chatter of inane comments accompanied by pauses where she snapped off selfies like she was an up-and-coming social media influencer.

"Ooh, I'm not sure this lighting's the best. What do you think, Billie? Do you reckon it makes my fake tan look too yellow?" Stopping dead in the doorway, thereby blocking anyone else from either exiting or entering, Stacey flicked her head back and forth, studying the image in her mobile.

"I think you need to move. Why not try a couple of snaps at the table? Candlelight is supposed to be romantic, and very flattering to the complexion," said Billie.

"Perfect." Stacey grinned at Billie, finally moved from the doorway, and surged across the room while she fluttered thick black lashes in Kirk's direction. "Let's get a really romantic shot of the two of us."

Kirk disentangled himself and lunged towards the table where the other members of the cast waited. Greeting everyone he pulled out a chair, waving a hand at Billie to sit but was foiled as she sent him a cheeky grin, choosing a seat between a silver haired older gent and a woman around her own age. Foiled, he subsided in the chair while Stacey motioned to a couple of people to shift themselves so she could sit beside him. There was a bit of general commotion as everyone shuffled about, dragging their chairs over the floor then a waitress appeared to slap a file of menus on the table saying the *'specials'* were noted on a blackboard near the counter.

Kirk looked about him. Only one table was vacant and even it had a Reserved sign. There were several families, a group of pensioners squinting at menus and one or two young couples giving Kirk the impression that the pub was very popular with the townsfolk. Disco music blasted from an adjoining room, terminating the tranquil atmosphere of the eating area. Several women screeched with laughter and a helium pink balloon trailing several long strands of multi-coloured ribbons floated into the room.

Ignoring Stacey who had turned her attention to fussing over the positioning of the lit candles which made up the centrepiece of the table, Kirk looked over at Billie but she had turned away.

"Natalie, great to see you." Raising her voice, Billie leaned forward and smiled at the man beside Natalie. "Troy, I see you've been roped in to help too. What characters are you two playing?"

Natalie smiled warmly. "I play Baxter's mother." She jerked her chin towards the end of the table. "He's the very good-looking young man with the sulky mouth. Troy isn't in the play. He's in charge of the lighting and special effects."

"What about you, Professor Callen?" said Billie looking at her other neighbour.

The silver fox puffed out his chest and said in his fruity deep voice. "I'm the butler."

Billie laughed. "Of course. There's always a butler."

"Exactly." Kirk grabbed the opportunity to interject

and steer the conversation forward. "Do you know everyone here?" When she shook her head, he rattled off names, indicating with a jerk of his chin who he referred to as he went around the table. There was Baxter whose last name Kirk couldn't recall, next to him was AJ Donaldson the local police constable, who was also playing a policeman. Next was Mrs Pamela Brown with the role of the family matriarch, his sister Pixie who was a maid, Marsha Wang, the victim's older ex-girlfriend and finally, a bubbling over Hester Beasley who would oversee hair and makeup and was clearly thrilled to be taking part. "I play the role of a bumbling detective, think Inspector Clouseau in the Pink Panther and Baxter is the victim."

The victim, Baxter, hadn't bothered to even nod as he was introduced, apparently far too busy scowling at his mobile.

"Then it's a murder story not a mystery?" Billie asked.

Kirk shrugged. "Both really. It started as a mystery and then somehow morphed into a murder story."

"And the pudding?"

"The missing pudding kickstarts a series of events that culminate in the murder."

"Okay," Billie said slowly, and Kirk experienced an insane desire to lean over and kiss away her tiny frown.

Stacey snuggled into his side – far too close for comfort, blew a kiss towards her phone, took another of those damn selfies, this time catching him in the frame.

Wishing someone else had put their hand up for the leading lady role, Kirk said in a rush as he smiled around the table, "This meeting is about ensuring everyone is au fait with what's expected of them, any questions or issues that anyone can see may crop up, working out the schedules for rehearsals, finalising the lighting, costumes, and the sets." Taking out his own mobile, he opened the Notes app. "I also want everyone to get acquainted now as we'll be all working closely together over the next couple of months. Apart from making a bunch of money for the charity, I want this to be a fun experience for everyone. Think of it as more like friends having a good time."

Snap went Stacey's phone.

Tap, tap, tap went her fingers as she sent the image out into the world.

At the end of the table, a mobile pinged signalling a text had been received.

The skin at the back of Kirk's neck tightened. He glanced up, opened his mouth to object but it was too late.

With a savage thrust, Baxter flung himself out of his chair, sending it flying before storming out of the room, mobile clenched in one hand.

"What's gotten into him?" Kirk stared after the younger guy.

Natalie said wryly, "I'm guessing no one mentioned these two..." Here she paused to wave towards the retreating guy and a smug-looking Stacey before continuing, "...used to be an item until Baxter took up with Stacey's best friend three weeks ago."

Wonderful. They had barely begun and already the cracks were showing. The next few weeks were going to be gruelling. Rubbing a hand over his chin, and wondering whether it was too late to recast, Kirk glared at the young woman. "What exactly did you say to him, Stacey?"

Tossing back her golden hair, Stacey turned a triumphant face towards him and revealed an obviously photoshopped image of the top half of a naked Stacey with Kirk's face looming over her shoulder. "Didn't have to say anything. I just showed him what he's missing."

And to his horror, she then handed her phone around so everyone – including Billie – could see.

Chapter Five

Crumbling the remains of her cupcake, Billie reflected on how much her parents had been through these past years and how little support she'd given them. There were no excuses. Apart from fleeting visits for their birthdays, she'd had blinkers on; her focus had been on building up her business and living the life she'd dreamed of since she was a little girl. She'd believed wealth would not only bring her happiness, but it would also fulfil her. She'd wanted the prestige of success, the dream house, the flashy cars, the perfect man. Well, she'd well and truly fallen short with the latter! He certainly glittered, with his charm, and surfer blond good looks. But he wasn't gold, although for eight years she'd believed he was the one for her. How wrong she'd been - on so many counts.

Her gaze travelled over the familiar contours of the vicarage where she'd spent the first eighteen years of her life. The harsh morning sun revealed how the aging boards once painted a pale green had faded to a dull grey. The guttering was rusted here and there. The lawn was more weeds than grass. But the house sat like an old buddha, comfortable, solid, dependable. Musk pink gauzy curtains hung in the windows, pot plants over-flowing with brightly coloured annuals were crammed on the front veranda while the windchime she'd made for her parents when she was twelve still dangled in pride of place, tinkling with each puff of the faint breeze.

A sense of contentment settled deep in her heart, and that restless urge to be somewhere else, to seek out that *something* she'd thought was lacking in her life, vanished as if it had never existed. Pity it had taken her almost forty years to realise where she truly belonged.

Turning, she met her mother's worried eyes. "I'm glad I'm home. Initially I thought I'd only be here a couple of weeks while I work out how to salvage my business."

"Have you decided what to do about that?" Florrie tilted her head.

Billie frowned thoughtfully. Her pet bird, Chompers, gave her bare arm a lick with his tiny pink tongue then strutted along the edge of the table. "For some reason, it doesn't seem to matter as much anymore. I didn't realise how much I missed this place until now."

She was having morning tea with her parents under

the gazebo she'd built for them, a few weeks after she'd moved back home, keen to give back when they'd asked no questions, simply welcomed her home with open arms and gentle smiles. The timber posts and rafters had been painted white, and she'd screened the roof section with cream coloured shade cloth to provide relief from the sun until the grape vine she'd planted took off. With the old natural toned cane furniture and bone-coloured pavers beneath their feet, the area was surprisingly inviting. Her parents had loved the results, sometimes they now had dinner out there in the cool of the evening. Despite the new gazebo being positioned in the front yard and in full view of anyone coming down the street, the setting was peaceful. Maybe it was something to do with being home, surrounded by memories and being with people who could be counted on, Billie wondered as she dabbed at the cake crumbs with a fingertip, then swiped up a dab of icing into her mouth. Picking up another cake, she tore off a small portion and nudged it towards Chompers. The cockatoo pecked away with gusto. "In almost twenty-two years I only visited you and Dad a handful of times. I should have spent more time with you. I should have come home sooner. I'm sorry, Mum."

"Hush now. Your father and I wanted you to live your life on your terms, and honey, it would have made no difference to the outcome. You know that," her mother said firmly, handing over a cloth napkin. "You're here, and that's all that matters."

"Still – I could have supported you more, Mum. I imagine, it hasn't been easy." She searched her mother's eyes while she wiped her sticky hands.

"That's true. I took ages accepting Jonas wasn't going to get better. I kept hoping. Praying." Florrie shook her head sadly, blinking away a few tears. "If it hadn't been for Edwina and Pam, I might still be living like an ostrich."

"I don't believe that. You're made of strong stuff. And you have this way of looking at life, like you can cut through all the crap and see what really matters."

"Oh honey. I'm guessing you're talking about Sawyer."

"I suppose." Billie's lips tightened and for a moment she had to fight the savage twist of hurt welling in her chest. But then the pain ebbed leaving behind something close to acceptance.

"Not all men are the same."

"You never liked him."

Florrie paused, as if choosing her words. "I wanted to, very much so. For your sake. It wasn't anything I could pinpoint but both your father and I never thought he was the man for you."

"For the first four years, I truly believed he was the one. We both loved surfing, and he proved to be a good business partner, great at reeling in more customers. He said all the right things to me – all the stuff a woman wants to hear."

Florrie shook her head and tutted. "Some men are

born knowing how to talk to a woman. Unfortunately, it doesn't always mean they're sincere."

"Too right. I learnt that the hard way when he began to spend not just hours but days away from me. I thought at first there was another woman. In some ways, I think that might have been easier to face than knowing he'd taken me for a fool. It's so annoying when your parents are right." Billie attempted a rueful smile and found to her surprise that it wasn't that difficult to find the humour in the situation. She looked up and met her mother's concerned gaze. "You know what, Mum? A second ago, I was feeling all this angst about how he let me down and ruined my life; and the utter humiliation of discovering just how long he'd been betraying me while I was oblivious. But now...I dunno. It's as if the whole debacle doesn't matter quite as much as it used to."

"I'll let you into a secret." Smiling, Florrie leaned closer. "It's this place. Bindarra Creek. I've always thought there was a special magic here. Perhaps, for the First Nations people this area was a place of healing and their memories and experiences have seeped into the land."

Billie set her teacup onto the saucer. "It's possible and wouldn't it be lovely if it was true?"

"Absolutely."

"Although, Dad..."

"I know, honey. I know. But he's here today. With us."

As if he wanted to remind them exactly that, a timely snort came from where her father dozed on a sun lounger, his battered cloth hat covering his face.

"Yep. Definitely with us," Billie added and smiled.

"It could be worse. We must look for our blessings wherever we can find them. For me – it's always been my family." Her mother winked. "And being surrounded by great friends and a caring community."

Billie rolled her eyes as she remembered what had happened the previous day, and grumbled, "Auntie Edwina keeps trying to grab my hand. She's positively anal about it. Can't you tell her to leave off? I don't believe all that palm reading stuff, anyway."

Florrie's nose quivered, her eyes gleaming with suppressed amusement. "I can't perform miracles, honey."

Billie laughed. "Good one, Mum. You being a vicar and all."

"Edwina means well." Florrie poured herself another cup of tea and waggled the battered old teapot at Billie.

"And nosey as hell. No thanks, Mum. I'm almost swimming with tea." Billie patted her full stomach while thinking with pleasure of her purchase of a china teapot with matching sugar and creamer. She'd already repaired the lid, taking her time as she'd wanted the cracks to be as unnoticeable as possible. The result had been better than she'd expected and now the set had been re-wrapped in tissue paper and stored in a box under her bed. All she needed to do was purchase Christmas wrapping paper and her mother's gift would be ready. She had still to decide on a gift for her father – something that was already giving her a headache just thinking about it. But she was sure an idea would occur soon.

"Don't forget what she predicts comes true a lot of the times. Oh, I could give you so many examples." Her mother leaned back in her deck chair and grinned as she looked along the road. "Speaking of Edwina's predictions – isn't that Kirk? I do believe he's heading for our home. I can't imagine it's me or your father he's coming to see."

"Mum!" She wafted a hand in front of her hot face. But no matter how hard she tried, she couldn't stop the welcoming smile on her lips as Kirk placed a hand on the gate and instead of opening it, bounded effortlessly over.

The showoff. But, gee he was a sight for sore eyes. That salmon-coloured tee moulded to a chest that screamed at Billie to run her hands all over it. And he had a way of swinging his hips just ever so slightly when he walked, that dried all the moisture from her mouth. Her heart began a heavy pound against her rib cage, her fingers curled, nails biting into the palms of her hands. She hadn't seen him since that – what she thought of as hilarious – episode at the Riverside pub where his leading lady had photo shopped a picture she'd taken of Kirk and herself before sending it to another cast member, causing quite a scene.

Although Billie and Kirk had texted a few times since the meeting at the pub that night, every message had been about the play and the sets she oversaw. Absolutely zero in regard to anything personal. What he did each day, who he was with, what he was thinking, feeling – all but consumed her waking thoughts. It was becoming harder to deny how often that occurred. But that didn't mean he had to know. This man wasn't a forever man. He was here today but she knew he'd be gone soon and would probably never even remember her name let alone her.

He moved closer, his intense gaze fixed on Billie.

Quickly, she snapped her mouth shut, hoping like crazy he hadn't noticed her gawping at him like a smitten teenager.

Florrie beckoned with a series of frantic waves. "Take a seat, Kirk. You're just in time for tea and cupcakes! Is that your new hat you mentioned? Now, you're a real Aussie cowboy. And a very handsome one."

Seriously, Mum!

But Kirk gave no indication of embarrassment. Rather his charming smile radiated nothing more than warm friendliness as he settled into a chair and tipped said tan Akubra back a tad from his forehead. "Good morning, all."

"We still haven't had the pleasure of your company at dinner yet."

"Sorry about that Mrs Miller. The play is taking up more of my time than I thought. If I'm not reviewing the script, I'm talking to people about lighting, costumes, even makeup."

"I imagine there is lots to do. We've bought our

tickets and both Jonas and I can't wait for the opening night. Maybe you should think about getting yourself a secretary." Here Billie's mother turned and stared at her daughter.

Said daughter could have slunk under the table and disappeared. Fixing a smile to her lips, Billie pretended an interest in the remaining crumb on her plate as Kirk winked at her.

Unperturbed her mother poured out another cup of tea and placed it in front of Kirk. "Nothing like a hot cuppa."

He stared at it for a few seconds then said, "Thank you."

"You don't have to drink it, you know. I can get you a glass of cold water from the fridge." Billie grinned, correctly interpreting his expression.

"Nonsense, Billie. Why wouldn't he want tea?" Florrie looked bewildered and pushed the plate of cupcakes across the table.

"Tea is fine." He smiled at them both and picked up a cupcake. "My favourite."

Billie indicated the cake in his hand. "I thought you were mad keen on scones and jam."

"Oh, I'm mad keen on a lot of things. You'd be surprised." He turned towards her, a gleam of something hot and glowing burned in his eyes.

Her breath seized and for one crazy moment, she had to force herself not to launch across the table and dive onto his lap. The need to taste his kiss was acute, it was like a physical pain. Aware of her mother's interested proximity, Billie counted to twenty and flexed her tingling fingers. The moment passed.

Looking smug, Kirk stuffed the cupcake into his mouth, a tiny grin playing around his lips, his cheeks bulging like a squirrel's. As if he'd suspected exactly where her thoughts had led.

Drat the man.

"Thought I'd check up on how you're getting along with the set," he said, after he'd finished enjoying his cake. "Mmmm, delicious, Mrs Miller. You could sell these and make a fortune." His hand hovered over the plate, while Florrie flushed with pleasure.

Chompers hopped across the table to stand beside Kirk's plate, flicking his head from one side to the other. He spread his wings wide and fluttered them, no doubt hoping to be rewarded with more cake.

Kirk scrapped a few crumbs towards the bird. "Does your skill run in the family, Mrs Miller?"

Florrie laughed. "Oh goodness me, no. If Billie had her way, she'd live off microwaved dinners."

As her mother and Kirk looked at her, Billie shrugged, grinning ruefully. "That's true. I can cook enough to survive, but that's about my limit."

"Pity. A man and his stomach and all that," murmured Kirk, sotto voice.

Florrie snickered.

Billie desperately sort to change the conversation then remembered why he was there. The Play. *Of course.*

"I've finished one backdrop and am about a third done on the second."

"Fantastic." Kirk clapped his hands together, startling Chompers, who squawked and flew into the air to land on Billie's shoulder. "Oh sorry. Didn't mean to scare your bird." He eyed the cockatoo who eyed him back.

"I'm glad you dropped by. I was meaning to phone and ask you to drop in. I need to know if what I've done meets your expectations."

"You could have called me any time. I'd have answered and been here like that." He smiled and snapped his fingers. "I respond straight away to your texts, don't I?"

Ducking her head, Billie fiddled with the spoon on her saucer, mumbling a grudging agreement. In truth, her hand had hovered over her mobile countless times, especially the last couple of days; longing to hear his voice, dreading to feel that mix of excitement and hope churning in her belly. And worse, wondering whether the younger and far more beautiful, Stacey had managed to capture his interest. From the gossip she heard via her mother and Tessa, the girl had him in her sights.

After draining the last of his tea, Kirk rose to his feet. "Let's look now, shall we? If you've finished your tea, of course."

"I'll just help Mum take the plates inside." She made to gather up the cups and saucers.

"No need. Anyway, I'm sure your father would like a cake or two once he wakes up." Florrie smiled as she settled back in her chair. "I'll sit for a while longer and enjoy the sun before rousing him for his tea."

"Okay, then, Mum. But give me a hoi if you need a hand." With Chompers clinging with his sharp nails onto her shoulder, Billie led the way around the back of the house to the shed her parents used for a garage. The doors hung drunkenly off their hinges, and the tin roof was rusted badly, but it was weatherproof making it the perfect place for her to work on the backdrops.

Flicking on the overhead light, she stood back, indicating the completed backdrop that still gleamed with slightly damp paint. It was a cheerful scene of an open fireplace with red and orange flames glowing in the grate, a decorated Christmas tree, a bulging timber bookcase and comfy wing-back chair. The 'wall' was painted a rich dark green which contrasted nicely with the bright colours of the fire, the pale cream of the armchair and the walnut toned bookcase. She'd also obtained a Victorian era side-table from Dodge, repaired the legs so it wouldn't collapse the first time someone placed a feather onto it, revarnished the timber and placed a chipped teacup and saucer on top of a doily positioned in the centre.

Releasing his grip, Chompers swooped over to land on the bench where he began to investigate the tins of paint, tapping his beak on the lids as if to check they were on nice and tight.

Kirk strolled up and down, leaning close to peer at some detail, straightening and then taking a few shots with his phone of the backdrop and then of the side-table. "This is excellent, exactly the right image I had hoped for, and the perfect colour tone for act 1. I love this table, too. Good job."

"How did you get on with obtaining more period furniture pieces?" Billie hand-fanned her hot face.

"I've nabbed this amazing chandelier which has tons of crystal dangly bits, a battered coffee table and two armchairs which are a lovely green and red checked pattern. Tessa and Dodge are on the lookout for a claw-foot bathtub for the bathroom scene." Turning, he examined the partly finished backdrop that was to be used for the second scene. "This is coming along well. I like the details that you've added on the bench here." His finger air-traced the plucked turkey and various vegetables she'd drawn, wanting to give the audience the impression of a real 'working' kitchen. "The lethal looking knife lying next to the turkey is a great idea. Yours?"

"Yeah, I thought it might be a good idea to have a couple of weapons hiding somewhere on the sets, since the play's a crime mystery. How's the cast getting along?" She held back a grin as she thought of *that* photo.

Kirk grimaced and rasped a hand along his jaw. "Civil is about the only way I can describe it, accompanied by a hell of a lot of glaring by a certain couple of people. I'm sure you know who I'm talking about. At least Baxter and Stacey have remained in the play. They're not half-bad for a couple of kids, Stacey especially when she isn't fooling about on her phone."

The words *'a couple of kids'* warmed Billie's heart. "Did she take down that photo?"

He nodded. "Apparently, she only sent it to Baxter, and she swears she deleted it."

Chompers ceased his lid checking, lifted a wing, and foraged for mites while Billie crossed over and pointed to the living room backdrop. "See here? That's a wrench lying on the top of the mantle."

"Hah! I didn't notice that. Very clever, Billie."

Shrugging, she tried to make out that his praise was no big deal. But she was kidding herself.

"Looks like I won't need to concern myself about the sets. However..." Kirk paused, his bright smile dimming as a worried frown appeared.

Folding her arms, Billie waited as an unwanted quiver wobbled her knees.

Kirk met her eyes with such an innocent expression, all her senses went into high alert. "It's the play. I'm not happy with several scenes. Not sure if it's the dialogue or the actions of the characters. But it would really be a huge help if you could come and give me your opinion. Now, I know that you have no experience as an actor but what I'm after is the audience perspective. Rehearsal is at seven. Tonight. I'll see you there." And without waiting for her to object, he disappeared out into the bright sunlight and was gone leaving her on fire with anticipation.

It took every atom of strength she possessed to remain standing in place and not rush to the doorway to gaze after him. Only a handful of encounters and already he occupied far too much real estate in her mind. And much to her dismay, his good opinion of her was a need she found difficult to dislodge from her heart. Her fingers curled tighter into her palms, her eyes closing as she dragged in several lungfuls of air, air that was still redolent with his fresh aftershave and which did absolutely nothing to quieten her racing pulse.

A few hours.

Only a few hours and she'd see him again.

She couldn't wait.

Chapter Six

Attempting to disguise how many times Kirk checked his watch by turning his back on the cast, no longer worked to quell their rampant curiosity. This was evident by how every member of the play standing about on the stage gaped at him while the younger members kept elbow nudging whoever was closest.

"Do you need to leave?" Mrs Pamela Brown folded her arms across her chest and pinned him with steely eyes.

The professor craned his neck to peer over the top of his spectacles as he gazed around the old cinema. "Expecting someone?"

At least three of them snickered.

Clearing his throat, Kirk rustled the pages he held,

aware that his face must be a tell-tale red since it felt like his skin was on fire. "Let's take it from scene five once more. Stacey, I want you to assume a shocked expression, possibly gasp after you say your lines, widen your eyes and then place your hand over your mouth."

"Mmmm, I thought I needed to portray shock or grief. It's my deadbeat husband lying murdered at my feet after all." Pouting, Stacey pointed at Baxter who had rolled over onto his side and was scratching his chin. The handle of the plastic prop knife stuck to the middle of his shirt with Velcro wobbled as he gave a gigantic yawn revealing all his teeth which he obviously hadn't brushed since the night before – if then.

A bit stumped, Kirk scrutinised the script in his hand. If Stacey had inferred that a totally different reaction was expected then perhaps he should review the scene. Could the dialogue be tightened? Tweaked so it was more comedic? Just exactly what the devil had he missed? He cast his eyes over the lines, telling himself this was a simple play in a tiny town miles from any discerning play critics or Hollywood scouts. He shouldn't be agonising over every little detail and yet, he wanted the play to be a success; more for the townsfolk than himself. Everyone he'd met had been welcoming, interested in discovering more about him, his family and friends, his life in California, what it was like living in the States. He'd been invited into people's homes, attended numerous barbeques and picnics and had been drawn into their lives. They couldn't have been nicer. If he could wrangle this script into something better than passible and everyone enjoyed the night, it would be his way of saying *'thanks folks'*.

He looked up to discover that the cast had taken advantage of his pre-occupation. Professor Callen was sitting in an armchair that had the stuffing leaking from it in several places. With his head back and eyes closed, he appeared to be catching forty winks. Baxter, still on the floor, had his mobile in hand, snapping off pics of himself. AJ, wearing an anxious frown, looked like he was memorising his lines. Natalie was bent over rummaging in a box for who-only-knows-what. Marsha Wang was talking in her high-pitched voice to someone on her mobile while Mrs Brown glared at Kirk, tapping one foot against the faded floorboards. And Mayor Donaldson had yet to show up, although given he had only three lines and appeared in a mere two scenes, Kirk wasn't that concerned with his non-appearance.

"What I want to know is when do we get our costumes?" Stacey turned to Kirk's sister who had her arms crossed, looked bored out of her mind, and who was playing the part of a housemaid, adding, "I can't wait to see what I'm to wear. I adore all those sequins and fringes."

Pixie gave a heartfelt sigh, pinching the folds of the black tank top she wore between two fingers. "I hope mine has lots of crystal beads and is black. I rarely wear any other colour. Kirk, any idea when our clothes will be ready?"

"A little while yet." Kirk smiled, tamping down his rising irritation, reminding himself he was working with people who had probably never acted in their entire lives. He knew for a fact that his sister had never been on the stage. With one rehearsal scheduled for each week, there remained, since it was already mid-November, only three more to go before play night. Boredom mingled with impatience already bounced off his team causing an acid burn of anxiety to chew away in his gut. What if – at the very last minute – one or more decided to up and leave? He'd be royally screwed. And with the slightest distraction sufficient to divert their attention from what they were supposed to be doing, or saying, it was becoming harder at each rehearsal to maintain their enthusiasm.

As for him, years of waiting on the sidelines while bit portions of a scene were rehearsed over and over had imbued him with hard-won tolerance. Nothing was achieved by a temper tantrum, mouthing off at others, or becoming irritated. The end result, a production that was polished to perfection, had always been his total focus.

He had to remind himself that these people were all volunteers, not professional actors. They were simply a bunch of everyday folk, who had either put their hands up to be part of something new, or because they'd been roused by the idea of helping others, or maybe because they had a secret dream to be on the stage. He couldn't blame them for not knowing in advance how much work would be involved or that the final practice was often the moment when they first got to see what they'd be wearing. It was up to him, the producer, director and writer all rolled into one, to marshal them on track.

And he had to be mindful, how much of a difference rehearsing in costume made to people's performance. It was if a new persona was born when you donned either culturally different clothes or period clothes – at least, that always worked for him. Snatching up a pen, he scribbled a note. Better check on the C W A ladies' progress in that regard as soon as they finished for the day and see if he couldn't hurry them along.

"Stacey, if you could start from the top of the page, please."

It took a few moments for everyone to stop what they'd been doing and pay attention. Stacey read her lines, gave a theatrical gasp then clapped her hand over her mouth so loudly, the action might well be heard at the other end of the room.

"Excellent, that's exactly what I'm talking about." Kirk beamed.

Poking her toe into Baxter's back, Stacey smirked. "Sorry hubby, looks like I'm not that broken-hearted about you dying."

Baxter rolled onto his back, linked his hands above his head and puffed out his chest. "If you were the one with the knife sticking out of her chest, I'd shed no tears either. But if it was Rachel, I'd be devo." He gave an insolent grin.

Shrieking, Stacey swept the plastic vase and flowers off the nearby coffee table and proceeded to whack

Baxter on the head, chest, anywhere she could reach. Pixie latched onto one of Stacey's arms attempting to wrestle her away from the laughing guy. The two other male members chortled, as Mrs Brown cried out in her stentorian voice, "Shame on you, Baxter. That's no way to behave. Your mother will have something to say when I tell her!" Even though Baxter was twenty-three if he was a day.

In all the commotion, Kirk didn't realise Billie had arrived until her cool voice piped up not that far from his left ear. "Don't tell me – this is part of the play."

"Do you think I should incorporate it?" Ignoring the chaos ensuing around him, he smiled, inwardly hugging the warm glow the sound of her voice and her sweet face infused inside him. It was as if every nerve end throbbed with renewed life and energy, and the gloom of the old cinema had lightened.

With one last mighty pummel of flowers, Stacey tossed the plastic vase onto the floor and stormed off, shouting, "I'm done here." Exit stage right.

"This is ridiculous. How much longer is this going to take?" Professor Callen demanded, rocking back on his well-shod heels.

Until hell freezes over if tonight was any indication, thought Kirk.

"I should go after her." But he made no attempt to move. If it had been up to him, he could have stayed there all day, just having Billie by his side was enough.

"Leave her to me. You had better help Romeo. There's blood on his cheek."

"Damn," he muttered, pushing aside personal thoughts as he leapt onto the stage.

By the time egos had been massaged, the set righted and everyone rounded up, another good thirty minutes had passed. At this rate it would be next Christmas before they were ready. Repressing a sigh, he asked Billie to sit in the audience and listen as they went through their lines, then told the cast they were to start from the beginning.

After a bit of moaning and groaning, a few rolled eyes as some muttered about the time, they began again. Amazingly, the play rolled along quite smoothly; admittedly though the cast were reading from their scripts. No one adlibbed and in Kirk's point of view, they seemed to have caught the comedic vibe he wanted to convey. But still, he wasn't one hundred per cent certain they had nailed it, and it was with some trepidation that he jumped from the stage to join Billie the second after the final lines were said which was when he summarised the case against the murderer and solved the mystery.

"Thanks everyone. Same time, next week?"

Goodnights were exchanged and the cast dribbled out the door, leaving Kirk alone with Billie. Taking the seat beside her, he leaned back against the hard frame, staring at the now dimmed stage. "Your thoughts?"

"I'm no expert."

"Agreed. But you're one of the masses."

"The great un-washed types?" Billie quipped.

Kirk grinned. "Exactly."

She laughed. "I enjoyed it. But there was a couple of places where the scenes didn't quite flow. Plus, I got a little confused about mid-way through the third act; when the maid and the matriarch were taking it in turns to hide the murder weapon."

"I knew it!" His mouth drooped as he rasped a hand along his jaw.

Billie placed a hand on his arm. "Hey. It's nothing serious. And I've got a suggestion or two. Not sure though that they will be helpful."

He turned towards her, his hand capturing her chin, his thumb sliding gently over her soft skin. "Nonsense. Your good opinion is exactly what I need."

Chapter Seven

A quick survey of her bank balance did little to lift Billie's mood. More than a week had passed since Dale Heighington, the new owner of Fred's Garage, had phoned with any offers of work. It seemed the people of Bindarra Creek were too busy getting ready for Christmas to concern themselves with servicing their cars. Hopefully, that would change soon. It had better or she'd be down to a big fat zero - dollar wise, leaving her with nothing to offer her parents for her food and board.

Almost forty and almost completely broke.

How had her life come to this?

With a sigh, she logged out of her account and cupped her face in her hands. Immediately, her thoughts winged back to that moment when for a few incredible beats, she'd been convinced Kirk intended to kiss her. Tracing her fingers over her lower lip, she trembled imagining the feel of him, the taste of him, the warmth of his body close to hers; and could have cried. Hungering for another man in her life was not part of her plans. But even now, although five days had passed, the impression of his touch lingered, igniting a torch that burned brighter with each passing hour. If she'd never fled to her hometown, she would never have met him. However that would have meant, she'd miss out on these precious moments with her father. And regardless of where the next few months led – if anywhere – that was something she could never ever regret.

Setting aside her phone, she pushed to her feet and turned to examine the stage sets with some satisfaction. At least, these were coming along nicely. Something to be grateful for. She'd been concentrating diligently on the sets over the past month, keen to have all of them finished well before the 9th just in case any last-minute adjustments or even an additional set might be required. All she had to do now were a few finishing touches and they were done. Picking up a screwdriver she moved over to the final backdrop, working hard over the next two hours without a break until she'd completed all that was possible at this stage.

Billie took a sip from her water bottle, wiping beads of sweat from her face with an old towel she kept handy. The heat inside the old shed could have roasted a chicken; the thick humidity caused her clothes to stick to her hot body. Through the open door she could see heavy grey clouds clustering near the horizon, although there was no breeze to stir the stifling air. But although clouds had been hanging around the region for several days, no rain had fallen. A little rain, no make that a decent downpour, wouldn't go amiss considering the surrounding land was so dry it was brittle to the touch.

With her mind no longer occupied by the backdrops, a certain guy popped up again in her thoughts. Smacking the bottle back onto the counter with a loud bang that woke Chompers from where he dozed on his perch, she exchanged her bottle for her phone. Her pulse quickened as the icon indicated several messages had been received while she'd been working.

And oh joy; two were from Kirk.

"Hey there."

It was as if he had materialised directly from her thoughts to the open doorway. His brilliant smile banishing the shadows from the dim shed; his very presence filling her world with colour and life. Try as she might, she couldn't stop her answering grin from spreading over her face.

"Thought I'd pop in and see how the sets were coming along," he said, advancing further inside the shed.

Billie wiped her damp palms along the side of her shorts, trying not to feel pleased as he raked her with an appreciative glance. "I've finished. What do you think?"

After a few minutes of checking them out, he gave her a thumbs up. "Excellent."

"Did you want something?" she blurted then could have kicked herself for the suggestive nature of her question.

Kirk opened his mouth then grinned as Chompers spread his wings and landed on Kirk's shoulder. Leaned against the bench, Kirk ran his forefinger over Chompers head, much to the bird's delight. "Tell me about this little guy. Have you had him long?"

She shrugged. "Dad bought him for my sixth birthday."

"Wow! I never imagined he was that old." Kirk's eyes widened.

"Yeah - both of us are practically senior citizens," she said drily then smiled when he laughed. "I can't imagine my life without him. He goes everywhere with me except I don't take him to the garage when I'm working. He stays home with Dad who I suspect has been sneaking him treats when I'm out of the way." Her eyes stung for a few seconds, but she blinked away the sudden moisture. "Chompers is doing good for his age, still plenty of mischief in him. Mitchell cockatoos can live up to sixty years in captivity."

Chompers, on hearing his name, preened, fluffing up the plumes of his bright yellow and red crest, hopping from one claw to the other, then trilled out a series of excited chirps.

"He's certainly stunning. I can tell you two are

close." He smiled as the bird shuffled closer to his ear and nibbled on a strand of his hair.

"He was very naughty when he was young. Chewed an awful lot of our furniture. Mum kept threatening to sell him while Dad would laugh and help me to patch up the holes. Hence the name – Chompers."

"Who's a beautiful boy," crooned Kirk, soothing down Chompers' soft plumage in such a way that Billie inwardly marvelled at how gentle and patient he acted with her pet.

Feeling more than a little vulnerable, she said gruffly, "You were about to say why you're here."

"Oh yes. Edwina tells me there's a competition each Christmas for the best decorated house and I wondered if your parents intend to enter. If so, I'd love to help fix your place up."

Whatever she'd expected him to say, that had never entered her mind. "That would be great. You can do the high stuff that requires a ladder, like stringing the lights from the guttering and around the new gazebo." Tilting her head to the side, she considered his equable expression. "Does your offer include the church? Mum mentioned the nativity scene needs to be erected and I've already offered to make some decorations for the pews."

"Sure. Why not." Then a quizzical furrow appeared between his brows. "Do you mean like a Christmas themed flower arrangement?"

"Mmmm. I was thinking more native grasses, twigs, pinecones, grevillea spikes intertwined with red and green ribbons rather than fresh flowers. We'll have to forage a bit. Go native." She grinned.

Kirk laughed. "Love it, already. Hey, is this a potter's wheel? I can't believe I didn't notice it last time I was here. Are you the resident potter?" He turned bright, inquisitive eyes towards her.

"Nah, not me. Although I might take a crack at it over Christmas when the garage is closed for a few days. This is for Dad. We picked it up a couple of days ago from Dodge's shop. It's like way old but does the job. Mum's been looking for something productive Dad could do that will also give him pleasure."

"How's that working so far?"

"Good. He loves it, although he's only used it a couple of times. Apparently, he studied art in university, in particular, ceramic production techniques, before he realised his life lay with the Church. I may be biased but I think he's got talent." She crossed to a cupboard and opened the doors, taking out a curved vase finished in a glaze of various shades of blues and flecked with silver glitter. "What do you think?"

"It's exquisite. I'll buy it off you and give it to Mom for Christmas."

"I'm sure Dad wouldn't take any money for it. You can have it for free."

But Kirk shook his head. "Nope. That vase would be worth a decent number of dollars if it was in a shop. Say, have you thought about selling some of his work?'

She shrugged. "Hasn't entered our heads. But it's a

great idea. He'll have to step up and make more though. So far he's only finished two vases and three mugs." She laughed. "There's a gift shop on Court Street that may take a couple on commission. I'll check with Mum and Dad first before I ask the owner."

Chompers let out a little trill of delight as Kirk petted him. "What do we do with this little guy?"

"I'll take him inside the house to his perch. He can spend a few hours dozing beside Dad."

"How is your father doing these days?" Kirk asked in a serious tone.

"Not so good this morning. He was very vague, believed he was still vicar and Mum had the devil of a time convincing him there was no service for him to perform today."

A couple of strides and he was beside her, his warm hand cupping her left shoulder for a couple of seconds. An act of solidarity that shook her to her toes. "I'm very sorry to hear that, Billie."

Unable to trust her voice, she nodded, holding out her hand for Chompers to hop onto then left the shed.

The next few hours were spent roaming the paddocks that edged the cemetery after which they moved along the riverbank. They soon filled the three sugar sacks Billie had found in the back of the shed, with their finds. To her amazement, there was laughter and an easy warm companionship flowing between them as they collected anything that could be used in the displays. Once she thought they had sufficient foliage, they returned to the shed at the back of the vicarage where she showed Kirk how to make wreaths using pieces of jute and strands of bright, shiny ribbons.

It was mid-afternoon when her mother strolled into the shed to inspect the results. "How lovely. Since you're already here Kirk, why not stay for dinner? I thought we'd do some snags on the barbie."

Billie chuckled when she caught sight of his confused expression. "Sausages cooked on a grill."

"Ahh." Kirk beamed. "Sounds great. I'm famished. Just let me text Mom so she can let Edwina know there'll be one less tonight." Taking out his mobile, he walked a little distance away and made the call.

Florrie picked up one of the wreaths. "How many have you made, hon?"

"Not enough for every pew, unfortunately. We can wait until we find more foliage if you prefer." Billie eyed her mother expectedly.

"I'd love to have some decorations in place by tomorrow if that's possible. We have a christening at ten in the morning. It will add a real festive feel to the occasion."

"No probs, Mum. Leave it with me."

"Us, don't you mean?" Her mother gave a sly smile as she looked over at Kirk.

Shaking her head, Billie laughed. "You're barking up the wrong tree. It won't be long, and he'll be back in the States."

"Edwina has high hopes of him."

Billie groaned and changed the subject. "Want us to assemble the nativity display today, too?"

"Oh please. And thank you." Her mother kissed Billie's cheek.

"Least I can do. You took me in again. You didn't have to do that."

"Oh nonsense, Billie. Your home is always with your father and me." She enfolded Billie in a warm embrace.

"What did I miss?" Pocketing his mobile, Kirk glanced at them both, his eyes sparkling with glints of brown, green and gold as they lingered on Billie.

"Girl talk," said Florrie, disengaging herself and wandering off with a satisfied smile.

"I like your mom."

"I do, too."

They grinned at each other.

Kirk began stacking the wreaths in a pile. "We've still got your house to decorate but there's plenty of daylight hours left before dinner. Shall we head to the church, first?"

"We will." She snickered then cringed; it sounded far too much like a wedding vow to be comfortable. But he gave no indication he'd caught the connotation.

Just as well. She must remember he was a here today and gone tomorrow kind of bloke. A man destined for stardom, with nary a small-town, white picket fence in sight. More like a mansion perched high in the Holly-wood Hills.

She sighed then forced her lips into a quick smile

when he sent her a thoughtful glance. The idea that he might guess how much she fantasised for something different, was too awful to contemplate. Better to stay focussed on today and this moment. Then pack away her silly daydreams, and decide what she intended to do with the rest of her life.

Chapter Eight

Hands stuffed in his pockets so he wouldn't be tempted to link his fingers with hers as he was uncertain whether she would welcome the gesture, Kirk strolled with Billie along the path that wound beside the Akuna River. He relived the wonderful hours he'd spent in her company yesterday, how much fun they had had together as they discovered bits and pieces of native foliage, made the wreaths, then decorated the old church. The day had cumulated in a leisurely dinner with Billie and her parents in the new gazebo as the sun set and crystal-bright stars played peek-a-boo amidst the clouds covering the night sky. All-in-all it had been a day he'd treasure.

If only she felt the same...

An hour ago, he'd sent a message asking her to meet

him by the river. When she'd ridden up on her bicycle, it had taken all his willpower not to leap forward and pull her into his arms. He'd soaked in her sweet smile, the faint sheen of perspiration on her skin and the trimness of her bare legs, tanned a light golden brown from the sun, and felt like he was living his most precious dream.

If only she felt the same...

The speckled shade from the massive willow trees lowered the scorching heat and high humidity of the day significantly and he smiled appreciatively. The willows' branches whispered softly in gentle sways with each puff of the faint breeze that fluttered over the river's surface. A platoon of ducks paddled by and further up the river, came a soft splash as a bird dived into the cool water. On the opposite bank, a small herd of five or so cows had waded into the river to drink. He wondered if he would spot a kangaroo and scanned both sides of the river with eager eyes. His new favourite pastime, checking out the local wildlife.

As if in tune with his thoughts, Billie said, "Wait another hour when it's closer to sunset and you might spot a roo or a wallaby."

Kirk gave a quiet laugh. "I can't help myself. I think they are so cute."

"They do have doe-like eyes and long lashes. It's a shame they can be a problem for farmers. But I have to admit, I agree with you. They are cute. But be wary around the boomers, that's the male roos, they can do some serious damage if you're perceived as a threat."

He felt the intensity of her glance as she turned her head to look at him. She was far too serious, and he longed to bring lightness into her life. He'd heard the rumours about her business going bust, and how some lowlife guy had betrayed her. Living with his Aussie relations the whispers had been difficult to ignore. But the truth of her circumstances was another matter, her past could be entirely different to what had been spread around the town. He hoped for her sake, that she hadn't been badly hurt by whoever had placed those shadows in her eyes, and the wall around her heart.

A wall he was determined to breach.

"Boomers, huh? You Aussies sure have a way with words."

"We also call them jacks or bucks." Billie grinned.

Kirk rolled his eyes. "I need a dictionary."

She pulled her gaze away and stared at the river. "So where are we going, exactly?"

Immediately, his amusement fled. "I want to show you something. It's further along the river, down near the fairgrounds."

"We call them showgrounds here."

He nodded. "Noted. When I was out for my run the other day, I took a different route, past this...showground area. There were all these people about and it looked like a refugee camp. That couldn't be right?"

"Yeah, nah." She swiped at a low hanging willow branch, pushing it aside. "I guess they *could* be termed refugees now that I think about it. Mum was telling me that since the restrictions were lifted after covid, the town has seen a steady influx of people. Some are travellers, just passing through. Others were looking for a tree change. Not sure if you use that terminology in the States." She sent him a questioning look.

"I know what it means."

"Well, like so many other towns in Australia, we've been unable to keep up with the housing situation. Unfortunately, rents have risen dramatically in some places. So we have a mob of people kinda squatting in town and on the fringes of the national park. They either can't afford the rent, or they've been unable to obtain somewhere to live. Even the caravan park is chockers." Her eyes narrowed as she frowned. "Hey, wait a minute. I thought the profits from the play are going towards the homeless. Wouldn't you know all this already?"

"I did know, at least, I had read about it online." Shifting his hands from his pockets, he spread them wide. "I didn't realise the problem was also in my own backyard."

"No place is spared, these days," Billie said glumly. "It must be a terrible situation to find yourself in."

While they had been talking, they had rounded the bend in the river and now stood looking over the narrow rough field that spanned in between the river and show-ground, delineated by a post and rail fence running the full length of the boundary. A small tent city had been pitched along the riverbank interspersed between a few caravans. There were also several campers and motorhomes of varying sizes, and even a few cars with awnings tacked onto the sides that provided some shelter from the elements. They were parked in a haphazard fashion on the yellowing grass. A couple of kids were playing in the shallows of the river, watched over by a group of adults sitting on towels. A dog barked nearby competing with music from a radio. Despite the upbeat tune, the atmosphere was leaden, filled with a weariness that drained the soul.

"Come on. I don't want to look as if I'm spying on them." Taking her hand in his, he tugged and together they walked back the way they'd come. Sunlight danced over the water like molten gold, and he was thankful for his hat and sunglasses to dilute the glare. To his hidden delight, Billie made no move to wriggle her hand from his, rather she appeared to be content to remain as is, their fingers interlocked, hands swinging as they walked.

He was making progress.

"Thanks for bringing me here. I hadn't realised there were so many people free camping," Billie said.

"I wish we could do something to help."

"Well, we are. The play, remember?"

Clearing his throat, Kirk looked at her. "Sure, but I wonder if there isn't more we could do to make this Christmas a little special."

"Mmmm. You're right. There *has* to be something. I'll speak to Mum. She and her cronies are bound to come up with a brainwave or two."

He tapped his finger against the side of his jeans,

thinking hard then said, "What about the markets that run on the first Tuesday of every month? Could we organise a special night market – just for one night for example – where people donate stuff that we could sell? All the profits could be used to make up small gifts for these good people. Something special. Wouldn't have to be big, something that would make their Christmas a little brighter."

"That's a fabulous idea!" Her voice thrummed with enthusiasm as she squeezed his fingers. "Mum told me the C W A, with funds donated from the council, are organising a hot meal on Christmas Day. And we could distribute the gifts early on Christmas morning! I love it, Kirk. It's such a thoughtful idea. We'll need to check with the council for approval, but I can't see the markets being a problem."

"Do you think we could pull it off next Thursday? Otherwise, we might run out of time, since Christmas Day is in about four weeks. That will give us a bit of leeway to give a call out for donations if we don't make sufficient money at the markets to cover costs."

"We could try but we'll have to move fast. Like start planning today." She shot a pensive glance over her shoulder back towards tent city. "You know something? If I hadn't had Mum and Dad to come home to, I might have ended up living in a tent myself. I read somewhere that all of us are only one event away from homelessness."

"But what about the business you owned?" He

slowed to a stop and turned to face her. There was such sadness in her eyes, he longed to wrap his arms around her and pull her close.

"After I sold the business, there was nothing left by the time I'd paid off the loans taken out in both our names." A tear spilled over and ran down her cheek. "I shouldn't feel sorry for myself, but I do. I was an idiot. I trusted my partner and he betrayed me."

"What happened?" He paused, mentally kicking himself. He'd spoken without thinking that she might not care to share with a comparative stranger. "You don't have to tell me."

"I want to." She looked him squarely in the face, gaze steady despite the sorrow emanating from her. "I loved that place. I'd saved so hard, worked so hard. It was every-thing I'd ever dreamed of owning, my own mechanic shop. And it was a success. People even came from Sydney to get their cars serviced by me and my small crew. All was on track. I was well ahead in paying down the business loan and had a house in Mereweather. Albeit I also had a mortgage." She gave a deprecating shrug.

"And then…" Kirk prompted when she fell silent.

"I met Sawyer."

Such simple words and yet he sensed they contained a wealth of information and emotion; hopes, dreams, probably even love. But definitely hurt and disap-pointment.

Billie dragged in a breath then continued. "I thought he was perfect, took him home to meet Mum and Dad. Although they said nothing, I sensed they weren't that keen on him. But I didn't care. For the next four years, I felt as if my life was complete. We spent our weekends surfing or volunteering as life savers. Our weeks we worked together building up the business. He acted so considerate and loving with me but gradually...I don't know...I began to feel something was wrong. That *he* was off. That he was hiding something from me especially when he disappeared for days at a time. I kept telling myself it was my imagination, that the perfect life I had built for myself was still perfect. I didn't realise that my life had been built on shifting sands until it was too late, and I lost everything. My house and the business had to be sold. You see, the man I thought I'd spend the rest of my life with had taken out loans and run up huge credit card debts in both our names to fund his on-line gambling habit. He was an addict, and I didn't see it. Maybe if I'd known, I would have been able to help him. Or maybe I could have reined him in somehow. If I hadn't been so blind, maybe I wouldn't have lost everything I'd strived so hard to achieve."

He squeezed her hands in silent sympathy for a moment, and she gave a wry smile.

"Don't feel sorry for me please. I was an idiot. Falling for a guy who had no substance, and way too much charm, and then on top of it, making him a full business partner with access to every aspect of my life and finances."

88

"No one is infallible." He tried to lighten the moment. "Even I have faults."

"Yeah? You don't say," she drawled, her eyes glinting with amusement.

"Indeed. My previous agent fudged the accounts and stole a good half of my earnings from the last soapie I starred in. It was only a chance remark by one of the other actors that made me hire an independent accountant to do a check. The next thing I knew, Robert was in Mexico and I was out of pocket and out of an agent." Leaning close, he placed a butterfly kiss to the side of her cheek then drew back, hoping he hadn't ruined the moment. "Thank you for trusting me with your situation. You didn't deserve what happened, and that guy didn't deserve to be with someone as special as you."

"Yeah, well. Ditto, I guess." She sounded breathless; a tiny pulse fluttered close to the corners of her mouth.

Was this the right moment to kiss her?

Devil take it but the last thing he wanted was to cause her to withdraw from him. Although he had to show he was serious about her sooner or later. Holding her gaze, he stepped in, intensely aware of every nuance of expression flickering across her face, of the anticipation dazzling in her eyes. His heartbeats thundered so hard his chest ached as need spiralled through his body setting him on fire. Capturing her hands, he drew her close. Her honeysuckle perfume embraced him, sending his head spinning. The feel of her warm, soft skin against his was more intoxicating than wine.

She moved.

He tensed; certain she would pull away from him.

But she nestled close, threading her arms around his neck, lifting her face towards him. Relief, exultation, pleasure was a tsunami he willingly drowned in. Dipping his head, his lips touched hers as the heat of the his passion consumed him. And just like that, he was lost to everything - but her - for all time.

Chapter Nine

Billie couldn't stop thinking about that kiss. For her, it was as if she'd been captured and inserted in a bubble where only Kirk existed and that one magic moment. Where the possibilities were endless. Her body yearned for his touch; her heart longed to re-live over and over the companionship they'd enjoyed these past few days. The problem was – could she trust her judgement?

Would he turn out to be all glitter and dross, like Sawyer?

Recently, she had begun to sketch out tentative plans to begin again in Bindarra Creek. She'd considered building up a new mechanic business by subcontracting to the local garage or sourcing her own clientele. She'd live a small-town life surrounded by family and friends.

Rationally, she reminded herself a love interest did not figure into these plans, she'd been there, done that and been well and truly burned. And yet, she couldn't quell the flame of hope burning bright inside.

Kirk – could he be the one?

The man who could be relied on through thick and thin.

The man who would never abuse her trust.

The very idea he could factor into her future was one that made her shake inside with a combination of joy and anxiety. Despite knowing his life lay half a planet away, her fantasy of a different future wouldn't be stifled.

That kiss had to have meant something to him, surely.

"Day dreaming – again – Billie?"

The teasing voice jolted her back to reality – her current reality which was working like a production line inside a broiling hot hall where the creaking fans did nothing to alleviate the heat baking through the tin roof and uninsulated ceiling. She looked over to meet Edwina Lette's amused gaze and smiled. "Have to keep my mind busy or I'll fixate on how hot it is in here."

The elderly woman's face crumpled into a million wrinkles as she scrubbed a linen hankie over her flushed skin. "Perhaps next year we'll do something about fixing the air-conditioning unit. But for now, we have to suck it up. There are others in a much worse situation than ours."

"Yes, of course." Billie didn't need the reminder. Her

thoughts had turned often to the people living in the make-shift tent city and how they would cope in the height of summer. She returned to gift-wrapping three organic scented soaps together with suntan lotion, a box of relaxing herbal tea and a small tin of chocolate biscuits, although she wondered what condition the chocolate biscuits would end up being after being trapped in the hot hall for a few days.

The man she'd been doing her best to pretend wasn't sitting beside her sorting through a haphazard pile of donations, enthused, "It's fabulous how much people have already donated for us to sell at the special markets tonight. And look, someone has donated a bunch of picnic baskets we can use to make up the hampers."

His arm brushed against hers and Billie's knees shook like jumping beans in a blender. "Agree. Auntie Edwina, the C W A ladies have outdone themselves this time. I can't believe you managed to organise everything in only a couple of days."

"Nothing to it. All it takes is knowing the right people to get things rolling. The baskets were donated by Holly David, she's quite the entrepreneur with her new business of gift hampers. She makes up picnic baskets too, sourcing local products like Pam and Beatrix's homemade wine." A spasm deepened Auntie Edwina's wrinkles as she drew in a sharp breath.

As if she had some kind of internal radar where her grandmother-in-law was concerned, Tessa appeared on the other side of the trestle table. Billie could have sworn she'd been on the opposite side of the room a second ago.

Tessa smiled at Billie and Kirk before saying, "Okay, Gran. You've more than done your bit for the day. Besides, I need your help at home for a couple of hours." Eyebrows arched, she waited impassively while the old lady, grumbling about being given orders, pushed a trifle unsteadily to her feet, then clumped around the table in her much-loved pink gumboots peppered with added stick-on glitter.

Her belly clenched as Billie noticed how Auntie Edwina didn't object when Tessa placed a hand on her elbow. Auntie Edwina had had more than one health scare in recent years and with her tricky heart problem, had been warned by her doctor to take life a lot slower. Even with her immediate family on close watch, that had been hard to monitor. Billie's faux aunt had always danced to her own tune.

"I hope the old gal is going to be alright." Kirk was also watching the two women leave the hall at a casual pace with Auntie Edwina shouting out instructions or advice left, right and centre, Tessa urging her forward and not allowing the elderly lady out of her grip. "I've become quite fond of her."

"She's a corker and that's the truth." Billie took a long drink from her water bottle before leaning over to inspect the jumble of goodies on the table. "Is that...is that a telescope?" She pointed to where a black and silver object poked out from beneath a layer of different size towels.

Grinning, Kirk pushed aside the linen and picked up the device with a slight grunt. "I believe you're correct. There's a few scratches in the paintwork along the scope and one of the legs has snapped off."

"Wow. That would make a perfect Christmas present for Dad. How much do you think I should offer for it?"

"But the leg?"

"Not a problem. I'm a fixer. Remember?" She beamed, her heartbeats quickening when his answering smile spread like sunshine over his face. Approval glowed hot and pure in his eyes.

Kirk shifted the telescope this way and that, then squinted down the scope. "Since it's damaged, would fifty dollars be a fair price?" His voice radiated doubt.

"I'll check in with Mrs Brown and...hang on. There's a tag attached. Says...donated by Gloria Donaldson. That's the mayor's wife. I'll send her a message and see if she has a figure in mind for what it's worth. I saved her number in my mobile after I serviced her husband's car the other week."

"Good plan. Hey, there's a zip-lock plastic bag taped to the side," he said before ripping the bag open and inspecting the contents. "Must be your lucky day, Billie. There's a bunch of spare lenses or maybe they're different filters."

"Oh, that's awesome. Good job, Kirk." Billie crowded close to his warm body, leaning over his shoulder so she could get a better look. His spicy after-shave filled her nostrils with every breath she inhaled. His body...damn, he'd tensed as if he expected...

"No canoodling on the job," barked Mrs Brown stomping towards the table, a towering pile of bulging plastic bags in her arms which she promptly dumped in front of them. "There's work to do if we want to get these stalls ready on time."

And then, amazingly, she winked at Billie just as she went to tramp off again no doubt to hector someone else.

This is what comes from people knowing since the moment you were born. Still, it wasn't irritating. Rather comforting if a tad embarrassing. Hoping Kirk hadn't spotted the wink, Billie leaned back in her chair, fished out her mobile, holding it under the table as if she was a schoolgirl and in class. "I'll make that call. You keep busy."

"I'll do the work of ten men," he quipped solemnly, the flecks in his eyes glowing like molten gold as he performed a classic body-builder's stance with his arms, showing off his firm biceps. His lips twitched at the corners as if he was desperately trying to hold his smile in.

Billie's face heated. He'd seen that wink.

The moon that night hung low to the eastern horizon, while to the west the night sky was dark with nary a star to be seen. Although the sun had set an hour ago, the heat still leeched from the asphalt and old brick buildings and lingered in the heavy, humid air. Despite the uncomfortable weather, the special markets were doing a constant trade. Perhaps the townsfolk preferred to be strolling down the quiet streets, enjoying the many decorated buildings rather than stuck inside their hot homes. Or perhaps they just wanted to be part of the fun. There were a lot of kids out, the teenagers ambling along in giggling groups, the younger ones with their families, many snapping pics with their phones of the colourful festive lights. According to her mother, a record number of people had entered the competition for the best 'dressed' Christmas house.

"It feels like there's a storm coming." Frowning, Billie stared upwards from where she stood behind the stall she manned together with Kirk and her father, who was enjoying one of his more lucid days.

Jonas sniffed the air, lifted his face then said, "Not tonight, love."

"How can you tell, Mr Miller?" asked Kirk, his voice warm with interest.

"I can smell rain a mile off. That, plus all this humidity hanging around usually means we'll be hit with a thunderstorm. But not tonight. No sulphur in the air, son."

Son. He had never called any of her boyfriends '*son*'. And on the few occasions they had met, his voice had never held that amount of warmth when he'd addressed Sawyer. Billie snuck them both a sideways glance as she bemusedly took money off Dr Maloof who'd purchased two well-loved teddy bears which she intended to use in the waiting room of her dental practice. Her gentle father spoke to Kirk with animation, his eyes clear and bright. They were now enjoying a discussion about his favourite boxer's last fight. She smiled. How wonderful. Both loved the sport of boxing. They had found common ground. Knowing her father, they could well end up talking boxing for the rest of the night. The sight of Kirk crouching beside the camp chair where her father sat and the way his expression shone with genuine interest tugged hard at her heartstrings.

The next couple of hours passed in a bit of a daze with her performing the majority of the selling and wrapping, and those two yakking away like a couple of boys on the way to a footy match. But they did stop and help pack away the stalls and the few remaining items that hadn't been sold into the C W A hall. They switched to baseball, which to Billie's astonishment apparently was her father's new-found pastime (watching American baseball on a streaming service) as they strolled through the quiet streets to home.

And as Billie approached the vicarage ablaze with bright Christmas lights hanging from the guttering, and twinkling fairy lights woven through the gazebo while a huge, blow-up Santa bobbed about the front yard, she savoured these few magic hours. They would be cherished for all time.

Chapter Ten

The play was going to be a disaster.

Kirk's name would be forever mud in this small town.

He was positive of it.

This was the final rehearsal before the big night, but it could have been the first. No one, apart from him, could recite one single line without having to refer to the script. Even AJ who Kirk had begun to think of as *'Mr Reliable'* stumbled his way through his few appearances on set. Stage fright had set in. Perhaps even the enormity of what they were about to attempt, had also finally set in.

And the result was not pretty.

Kirk's smile was tacked onto his face so rigidly that his jaw ached with the effort, as he said through his clenched teeth, "Stacey, try to inject some emotion into your voice. We want desperation, not boredom."

"I need a break. We've been at this for hours!" she moaned then flopped onto the armchair.

With a resounding crack, the damn thing broke into two, spilling her onto the floor where she landed on her backside. Her squeal sounded like a gutted pig.

Baxter roared with laughter. "Must be your big arse!" he spluttered which only made Stacey scream even louder. If that was possible.

Mayor Donaldson attempted to scrabble onto the stage from where he'd been watching from the front seats, all the while, bleating as he hoisted one leg, got nowhere, hoisted the next, slid back down, "My God! Is she hurt? Remember, the Council has nothing to do with this play! If there's an insurance claim, it's a private matter."

AJ rushed to assist Stacey to her feet, brushing at her person with his hands to remove the odd piece of chair-arm or foam stuffing clinging to her dress.

Stacey shrieked, "You're driving splinters into me! Ow! Ow! Leave off, you idiot!"

Face red, AJ dropped his hands and stepped back. Straight onto Baxter, rolling about on the floor still guffawing. He tripped. Went down hard.

Another crack.

Kirk made record time bounding to AJ's side. He lifted the white-faced guy to a sitting position, stared bug-eyed at AJ's twisted left ankle. "Somebody call for an ambulance!"

Mayor Donaldson clambered across the stage on all fours, his face almost as pale as his son's. *"AJ…"*

"Everyone stand back. I have my first-aid certificate." Mrs Brown knelt with a creak of her knees and with a gentle touch examined AJ's foot before lifting a serious gaze to meet Kirk's worried one. "I think it's broken."

Feeling drained to his soul, Kirk trudged back to Fig Tree Lodge after he'd seen one of his cast members bundled into an ambulance with a stressed out father beside him, another member bundled into her indignant parents' care and the rest hurrying off to their respective homes. What a disaster. A new chair would have to be sourced. Dodge could help there – hopefully he had something similar on hand. But the clincher, depending on how badly broken AJ's ankle was, Kirk might need someone else to step into the role. His phone buzzed which he ignored. Kirk didn't think he could handle another whining discussion with his agent about when he'd be Stateside. Running a hand through his hair, he wondered how soon he could contact the hospital to check on AJ's condition. He hoped for the young guy's sake that the break wasn't too serious and would mend well. AJ had been great to have on the cast, always obliging, never complaining, turned up on time and had been the first to memorise his lines (apart from tonight). He didn't deserve what had happened. If that fool Baxter hadn't been clowning around...

Maybe he could talk Billie into taking AJ's place.

Nope. That wouldn't work, not with opening night – the only night – a mere three days away. It would be impossible to get someone else up to speed. Although if he thought about how much of a hash the entire cast had made of the play at tonight's rehearsal, maybe it wouldn't matter.

They were doomed. And he'd wanted so much for the play to succeed.

His footsteps crunched loud over shrivelled leaves and dry twigs that littered the sidewalk following the several hours of savage gusting wind that had occurred earlier that day. The haunting hoot of an owl echoed, and Kirk looked to the night sky for some sign of the bird. He heard the heavy whoosh of wings but couldn't spot it. He inhaled, catching some lemony scent and something else he couldn't put a finger to. If Billie was here, she'd be able to tell him.

Immediately, the thought of her lifted his sagging spirit. He wouldn't give in. Defeat was not an option. They would make this play work and the night would be a success. At worse – well, everyone would surely have a fun time.

As if she'd sensed his low, his mobile buzzed, lighting up with her name. Smiling, he raised it and said, "Billie." Her name was so sweet on his lips. Like her, it was unique – at least to him.

"How did it go?"

He gave an exaggerated groan. "You don't want to know."

"That good. Wow, I'm impressed."

Her chuckles warmed his heart. "There was an accident." As he informed her of what had happened, concern washed over him once more. "I'm worried the guy might be seriously hurt."

"Poor AJ. You sound like you're walking home. If that's the case, how about I come round and we can go to the hospital together. We can keep his dad company while AJ has X-rays or whatever. No, hang on, I have a better idea. We'll go and pick up Mrs Donaldson first. She doesn't drive and I don't think their other kids are in town at the moment. I'm sure she'll appreciate the lift."

"Great plan. I love it." Kirk looked about him before giving her details of his location.

It wasn't long and she was pulling up beside him in her parents' car, an ancient sedan with an engine that purred and certainly didn't make any of those odd grating or grinding noises that his had been doing lately. He surmised that Billie had taken over the car's care upon her return home.

"Need a lift?" Her smiling face leaned out the driver's side window.

"My hero." When he'd fastened his seat belt, she moved off driving at a cautious speed along Willow Tree Drive before hanging a left then a sharp right and on over

Kingfisher Bridge where, faced with an open road, she put her foot down.

"The Donaldson's have a small property a few klicks out of town. Won't take long. I've already phoned Mrs Donaldson and told her we're on our way." Billie sent him a reassuring smile. "No need for us to explain anything, she's aware of what happened to AJ."

He nodded, relaxing into the seat and content to allow the warm night air from the open windows gently buffet his face.

"Where's your car?"

"When I cranked the engine this afternoon, there was this almighty bang and a bunch of black smoke blasted from the exhaust. I think it's broken," he said mournfully.

Billie chuckled. "Yeah. Sounds like it. I did warn you. You never know though; it might be saved. I'll look at it tomorrow if you like."

"Thanks heaps. You're a life saver."

She laughed again. "Would you believe that I *am* a life saver, or I was. I volunteered at a local beach when I lived in Newie."

"There is so much more to you than just a beautiful face," he mused, genuinely impressed noticing how her face flushed pink at his compliment. "I mean it, Billie. You truly are quite remarkable."

Leather squeaked as she shifted position. "I'm just like everyone else."

"Not to me." But if the frown wrinkling her forehead was any indication, she didn't believe him. What would it take to make her trust him? Her previous boyfriend had let her down badly; more than that, he'd destroyed her professional reputation as well as sending her business to the wall. The guy was a total loser and didn't deserve someone as special as her.

"Don't fret too much about the play," she said as she slowed the car before turning onto a graded road that wound past dark pastures towards where a house glowed with Christmas lights in the distance. "It will all come together. I'm sure of it. AJ can still perform even with a cast on his leg."

"You think?" Now it was his turn to frown.

"I'm certain of it. He was so chuffed when his offer to be part of the play was accepted. He'll give it his all along with the rest of them. Mrs Brown is a real trooper, she never lets the side down, same with AJ's dad, the Mayor. I know Baxter and Stacey act like a couple of young twits but their parents attend our church. Mum reckons they're solid, they'll ensure their kids behave themselves on the night. I don't know the Professor but I'm friends with Natalie and she and the Prof are good mates. They'll step up, too."

The car rolled to a halt outside a sprawling house with a wide veranda on all sides. A woman ran down the short flight of stairs as Billie reached out a hand and touched his. "And then there is your sister – and you. I've seen one or two episodes of that soapie you starred in.

You'll ace it, Kirk, and the play will be a winner just you wait and see."

"I sure hope so, 'cause it would be awesome if we could make a real difference to someone's life this Christmas."

"We will."

Her faith in him caused his chest to swell with pride and an odd humility. He knew then that he'd never let her down. Taking her hand in his, he quipped, "We'll do it together – your magical sets and my amazing stage presence."

"See what I mean? Bindarra Creek is not going to know what hit them."

And they shared a broad grin as Mrs Donaldson climbed into the car's backseat, saying for all the world as if Billie was a taxi driver, "Ahhh right, hospital, please."

Chapter Eleven

Watching from the sidelines behind the heavy black curtain, Billie felt her chest swell with a mixture of pride and an odd pang she found hard to identify. Kirk had nailed the comedic detective persona perfectly. He owned the stage, his voice resonating with the right amount of confusion, and bafflement, aided by a fabulous supporting cast.

The audience listened spellbound, roaring with laughter without prompting, and gasping at the pivotal moment when the missing Christmas pudding was unearthed inside the stuffing of a wing-backed armchair. And then – the murder weapon was discovered inside an ancient text on herbs and poisons where certain references had been highlighted by Baxter. Apparently, the victim had thoughts of doing away with his new wife. In a grandstanding finale, Kirk stumbled his way through reiterating the clues to then denouncing the murderer as none other than his own constable, who had been in love with the victim and became enraged when he had taken a wife.

It was obvious that Kirk had talent in spades. Surely it wouldn't be long before he was winging his way back to the glittering world of Hollywood and stardom. Which meant, fantasising about a relationship with him was a waste of time should he decide to return to the country of his birth. No matter how hard she tried she couldn't visualise herself living half a world away; not now. Coming home to Bindarra Creek had been like peeling off the second skin she'd worn for so long, she'd forgotten her true self. She loved this small town, loved the people, loved the beauty of the surrounding countryside, the rich scents of the Australian bush. This place was in her blood, it grounded her. Besides, she wouldn't leave her parents, her need to embrace all that family life had to offer was too great.

But should Kirk decide to stay...

There - she'd finally admitted how much she longed for that to happen. The crowd gave a tremendous roar accompanied by whistles and wild clapping. With a start, she realised all the cast members had hurried back to the stage and were taking their final bows.

Then Kirk held up his hands for the audience to quieten before announcing his appreciation for their enthusiasm, thanking his fellow cast members and then going on to thank all the volunteers who had worked so hard behind the scenes. When he said Billie's name, he turned and looked directly at her.

And smiled.

A smile that was so different from every other one he'd granted her.

A smile that inflamed her blood while at the same time wrapped around her heart with a reassuring tenderness. Her eyes burned, his image blurred as her throat constricted. What did that smile mean? Did it mean anything at all?

She blinked and he came into focus once more.

However, he no longer looked at her, rather his attention was on his cast, laughing at something Stacey whispered into his ear. The cast took another bow, trooped from the stage via the opposite exit, and she stood alone.

A cold emptiness chilled her veins and she shivered.

"Wasn't that great?" Tessa Myer's excited voice sounded beside her.

Pulling herself together, Billie smiled. "Loved it."

"Come and join the others. There's a bit of an impromptu party going on in the reception area for the cast and us over-worked volunteers." The younger woman's voice was steady, but there was warm sympathy in her dark eyes.

Billie nodded. "Sounds good. Any idea how much the play made?"

"Dodge is still tallying up the figures, but he thinks it could be well over a thousand at least."

"Excellent news! Now, where's that drink with my name on it?"

"Ready and waiting for you. Come on." Tessa linked her arm through Billie's and together they followed the last stragglers dribbling out the exit doors.

When they reached the lobby area of the old cinema, it was obvious some of the audience had also decided to join in the celebration. The restricted space hummed with energy and lively conversation. She waved to Abby, who was the town's senior police constable, and Roman standing with their two adoptive boys, Drew and Eddie. Drew still had the video camera in his hand which he'd used to film the play. The proud expressions on Abby and Roman's faces told it all – the boy had done a good job. At some point over the weekend the play would be available for anyone who wanted to watch. Before the play had begun, Abby had confided that Drew had been anxious over the responsibility he'd been given however he'd received a lot of advice from Sean Stevenson, a new guy in town and who had been tutoring both boys after school.

By dint of ducking and weaving, they eventually made it in one piece to where the ticket counter had been transformed into a makeshift beverages' dispenser. Dodge stood behind the counter with his Gran and Warren, his father, all busily handing over either hot cuppas (with hot chocolate available for several children milling about), cold beer from a couple of eskies crammed with ice and cans, or plastic glasses of wine. Young Tilly, all but jiggling in her sparkling shoes at the excitement of being allowed up way past her bedtime, stood on a plastic chair offering cardboard straws to those who wanted one.

"Great turnout. The sets you made Billie really made the show." Dodge handed over a glass with a broad grin.

Billie sniffed the contents, then sighed. Perfect. She raised the glass in a toast and took a sip of the home-made blackberry wine before answering. "Kind of you to say, thanks mate."

"Hits the spot?" His eyes crinkled with laughter.

"Ooh yeah." She inspected Tilly's outfit, hiding her amusement as the little girl swished the beaded hem of her purple, nineteen-twenties dress and preened. "Love that dress, Tilly."

Tilly's expression as she looked at her great grand-mother was loaded with adoration. "Grannie and I have matching outfits."

"I noticed," said Billie, smiling.

"And here's the man of the hour. He sure has his timing down to an art," quipped her Auntie Edwina as Kirk shouldered his way through the throng.

"Hey all. What did you think of the play?" Although the question was aimed generally, Kirk's gaze latched onto Billie and lingered.

Aware of how the others flicked their eyes back and forth between her and Kirk, she did her best not to reveal the sheer pleasure the sight of him induced. No one spoke, obviously waiting for her to respond first.

"Good. But I'm no play critic."

The others gasped except for Auntie Edwina who snickered.

Hurt flickered across his face before his professional demeanour cloaked all emotions. "Please. Don't overwhelm me with your enthusiasm."

Face burning, Billie lifted her chin, already regretting her offhand words. "If that sounded as if I was disparaging you or the play, then I apologise. I only meant I'm no judge. I've only seen three plays in my life, and two of them were when I was in high school. For what it's worth, I enjoyed every minute."

Kirk smiled, captured her hand, and raised it to his lips. Still holding her gaze, he tenderly kissed her knuckles. "Your opinion, babe, is all that matters."

Her heart stuttered. If only he really did mean that sentiment. Desperately trying to maintain her composure and probably failing utterly, she mumbled, "Don't call me babe. I'm not a teenager and besides, I'm older than you."

"Are you really? I don't believe it."

She puffed out a loud breath while everyone around her grinned. Even Tilly was chuckling. "You would have had to be deaf to miss it when Auntie Edwina announced my age, and yours, as loud as possible. Right at the get go the first time she introduced us. You were standing beside her, so I know you know."

He gave a slow smile as he slowly released her hand. "I see you for who you are – and you're ageless to me."

Heat crawled over her skin as she met his intense gaze. All the air seemed to evaporate from the room. "Yeah, well, not really. What can I say? It's a gift."

He laughed and the sound was so engaging, a reluctant smile spread over her face. "Priceless."

Did he mean her? Or her comment? Too hard to determine. Plus, this conversation was way too personal considering they were not alone, even if they were surrounded by people who cared deeply for them. Longing to drag him outside and either devour him with kisses or demand an explanation, Billie wrenched her gaze from his and looked around the room. "Everyone is having a great time."

Accepting the change of topic, Kirk responded in a calm voice, "They sure are. I hope we made a decent amount for the charity."

Dodge spoke up. "I reckon a good two grand. We had a rush of last-minute on-line sales and Mrs Williams hasn't confirmed the amount yet. We should know the full total tomorrow morning."

Everyone grinned. Tessa clapped then gave her husband an enthusiastic kiss on the cheek. "Once we know the final figure, I'll announce it on the community social media pages."

A mobile trilled. Almost everyone reached for their phones.

"It's mine." Kirk grimaced as he recognised the name

on his mobile. "Sorry, folks. It's my agent. Do you mind if I take this call?"

"Go for it, mate," said Dodge while Tessa waved him off.

Auntie Edwina frowned as Kirk melted into the press of people, searching for a quiet corner, then turned towards Billie. "You need to go after him. Now."

"Gran!" groaned Dodge.

Tessa giggled.

"I'm not going to interrupt a private phone call. Excuse me. I'll see if either Mum or Dad would like a drink."

Dodge waggled a can at her. "Take this one, if you like. It's a low alcohol beer. Your Dad might go for it."

Auntie Edwina snorted. "More likely Florrie will but if they don't want it, I'll take it." Eyes narrowed, she glared at her grandson when he shook his head.

"No way, Grannie. You know the rules."

Huffing, she plucked Tilly off the chair, sat herself down with the child in her lap. "I'm on strike then."

"Good. You need a break."

Laughing, Billie left them to their squabble and went in search of her parents. Certain she had glimpsed her father's snowy wisps of hair near the entrance, she edged her way around the corner of the room only to come across Kirk leaning against the wall. *Bloody hell.* Now he'd think she'd followed him. She made to slip in between Mrs Brown, still resplendent in the last costume she'd worn in the play, and Roy Towns, perspiring in a shabby suit that was redolent of moth balls, but was too late. He'd seen her.

"Billie. Wait a moment, please," called Kirk before lowering his voice and muttering into his phone for a few more seconds.

Poised on the toes of her feet, Billie waited for him to end the call.

A moment later and he was beside her, a bemused smile lighting up his face. "That was my agent."

"Uh huh." Her heart skipped several beats as her belly went into free fall. Despite the heat of the over-crowded room, she shivered, her skin prickling with cold forewarning.

"She's got fantastic news."

Billie squeezed her eyes shut as if by doing so, she'd block the blow she sensed was heading her way.

"Are you okay?"

Her eyes snapped open to find him peering closely at her. She couldn't speak. All the words she'd wanted to say, wished she said, lodged hard and fast in the base of her throat. Besides, it was obviously too late to say anything at all. She etched his face into her memories, the fascinating glow of gold and green in his eyes, the gentle curve of his mouth, the firmness of his jaw. She'd never forget.

"Feeling sick? I'm not surprised. This place is like a furnace. Some fresh air might help. We'll go outside." Locking her fingers with his, he tugged her through the crowd.

They emerged onto the footpath where a few people stood around chatting in small groups. Still wordless, Billie stared up at the night sky, hoping for a star upon which she could make one last wish. The clouds that had threatened rain all day had disappeared, and the sky was a black curtain studded with glittering white crystals. Her gaze latched onto Venus, a brilliant flash of light in the darkness but before she could even think about her wish Kirk spoke.

"How are you feeling now?" His voice vibrated with concern.

She croaked out, "I'm good. It was the heat." And gave a weak smile that dimmed when matched against the brilliance of his answering grin as he stroked her fingers with his thumb. She mustered her courage. "What did your agent say?"

"I've been offered the lead role in a big-budget, action film. Deets are a bit sketchy, but they start filming in the New Year."

Too late to make that wish. "Congratulations." Hallelujah, she sounded like her normal self despite feeling as if something precious had been lost.

He hesitated, his smile dimming. "I haven't said yes though."

For one crazy moment, Billie thought he was uncertain of whatever he intended to say next. *What if...?*

Her parents hurried through the door, someone close on their heels. "Billie. We've been looking everywhere for you." Her mother sounded flustered. "Look who's turned up in town."

"Hello, honey. I've missed you so much. Forgive me. Please?" And there was Sawyer, blond hair shining beneath the beam of the streetlight, perfect smile in place as he took her limp hand from Kirk's and pulled her into his arms.

Chapter Twelve

Still uttering profuse apologies amidst a torrent of compliments on how charming he found the town, Sawyer hustled Billie and her parents into a nearby car. Head whirling, her ears buzzing, Billie kept wondering whether what was happening was all part of a crazy mixed-up dream. She felt as if she was floating above the ground, like she was having an out of body experience. Her fingers ran over plush leather, that was real enough. She looked at her ex as he settled behind the steering wheel and sent her a confident smile.

"Everyone comfy? Let me know if you need the air con colder." With only a cursory glance along the road, he pulled out and roared down the street.

"Where did you get the car?" she asked, her voice harsh, but sounding far away.

Her parents, seated in the back, didn't utter a word and in fact, had had little opportunity to say anything since Sawyer had monopolised the conversation since he'd expertly cut her away from Kirk.

"Rental, darling. How could I afford anything else?" The limpid gaze he gave her brought her hackles up.

She knew that look. Had learnt the hard way to recognise it.

He lied.

Which meant he had had secret funds squirrelled somewhere neither she nor the creditors that had howled for her blood, could find.

He was up to something.

But what?

The drive to the vicarage was short, made even quicker by the speed Sawyer employed. If she objected, he'd only drive faster. With a flourish, he turned into the drive and killed the engine. Billie scrambled out of the car, almost tripping in her haste. She needed to be somewhere else, somewhere far from his unsettling presence, somewhere she could think. Abandoning her parents to face Sawyer alone, she tore along the path and into the house. Chompers squawked indignantly as he was awoken more abruptly than he was used to when she snatched him and his perch near the kitchen window and charged into her bedroom. After setting down the perch close to her bed, she fussed over him, soothing his crest, tickling him under his beak but he fluffed up his feathers and turned his back. He wasn't used to being by himself.

Such a social bird, he lived for company but taking him to the play had been out of the question.

"Next time – if there ever is a next time – I'll get someone to sit with you," she whispered, her eyes stinging with tears.

What had promised to be a night to remember, had instead disintegrated into a nightmare. First Kirk's agent phoning then Sawyer turning up. Leaving her pet to sulk, she flopped face down on her bed, her fingers clenching over the too-warm bedspread. From the living room came the faint murmur of voices then the sound of the front door closing. She assumed that was Sawyer leaving. She waited but didn't hear an engine starting up which could only mean he intended to spend the night in his car. Footsteps padded along the hall, then the soft snick of her parents' bedroom door closing.

Silence settled over the old house.

Her belly roiled, nausea churning. She should go outside and tell Sawyer to get the hell away from her home but now she didn't want to even look at him. What *had* Kirk been about to say? What had been hovering on his lips before Sawyer had wrenched her into that unexpected embrace?

She rolled onto her back and scrubbed at her wet face with the backs of her hands, staring glumly up at the ceiling where, dimly lit by a lamp on the bedside table, glowed the constellations of the Southern Cross and Orion's Belt. After all these years, her parents had never removed the glow-in-the-dark stickers they'd placed there when she had been a child. Somehow that realisation caused fresh grief to grip her by the throat. Choking, crying, she whipped out her pillow and sobbed into the soft cotton slip.

She didn't know what hurt the most; Kirk's stunning announcement that Hollywood had made him an offer, Sawyer arriving with his poisonous presence, or her parents still clinging onto the remnants of her childhood.

The storm of emotions passed leaving her limp, depressed and tired. Tomorrow she'd give Sawyer his marching orders before whatever scheme he had cooked up dragged her parents into his seedy world. Because she was certain he would never have popped up in her life again unless he wanted something. He was probably up to his eyeballs in debt and hoping to con her parents into bailing him out. Well, that was *not* going to happen.

She'd ensure he was out of town before he could begin to spin his cobweb of lies even if she had to go to the police and request a restraining order. Even if he was genuinely remorseful over the way he'd acted and wanted to make it up to her, her feelings for him had changed. Someone else now lived in her heart.

Once rid of Sawyer...

Could she...

Dare she hunt Kirk down and demand to know what he had intended to say?

Or should she accept the inevitable – that his future lay a world away. And really when she thought about it, should she even try to change his mind? Kirk deserved the best of whatever life could give; he was kind – look how sweet and considerate he was with her father. He was generous – giving up his holiday to work on a play for charity. Obviously loving. She'd had plenty of opportunities to witness his warm relationship with his mother and sister and how fond he'd grown of Auntie Edwina and the rest of the family. Funny, maddening, and oh so bloody attractive. Sure he had charm, the same easy charm that characterised Sawyer.

But Sawyer's glitter was all dross while Kirk was solid gold.

Pain spiked across her forehead. Too many things to think about, too many maybe's and what if's. What she did need was a good night's sleep. Perhaps her life wouldn't look like such a disaster in the fresh light of day. With that thought, she shut her eyes, hoping and praying for oblivion for a few hours. What she got however, was a restless night, tossing and turning on hot sheets and aching for a man who in a few weeks' time, might never even remember her name.

The old cinema was stuffy, the air stinking of stale deodorant and perfume causing Kirk to breathe through his mouth as he packed the last of the props into a plastic tub and secured the lid. Without the sizzle of heightened nerves, the bustle of people scrambling in and out of costumes, the hum of anxious whispers, the backstage area was bleak, the silence leaden – exactly matching how he felt. He hadn't seen or heard from Billie since that heart-stopping moment when she'd embraced another guy six nights ago.

Not just any guy.

The guy.

The one who had broken her heart. The one who had pleaded for forgiveness in front of him, Billie's parents, and the folk gaping at the drama unfolding before their eyes. The one who begged to be given a second chance.

It was enough to make a guy want to punch someone.

Someone in particular.

Since that wasn't an option and he'd always gone by the belief that violence was never the answer regardless of the circumstances, he'd spent the days jogging, working out in Dan's gym at the back of the Riverside Hotel and helping move old furniture around in Dodge's store. Anything to keep busy and avoid making a decision that would affect the rest of his life.

In other words, he had yet to accept the lucrative offer that could path the way to stardom in Hollywood. Poor Cristina, his agent, didn't understand why he hadn't leapt at the opportunity. How could he explain that he was tempted to toss it all away for the sake of a pair of blue eyes that radiated an integrity and guarded sweetness that had melted his heart?

To walk away from Billie was an option he didn't

want to contemplate. But now Sawyer was back in her life, where did that leave him? Staying in this small town and watching them together was too high a price and one that he wasn't certain he could pay. He'd set himself a test – tonight he'd attend the Christmas Carols to be held in the local showgrounds, force himself to go up and be pleasant to the happy couple. If he was able to hang around them and not feel as if he had his soul ripped from his body, maybe he could stay in this vast country and make a new life.

Maybe.

Or maybe one more meeting with Billie would give him the closure he needed and he'd be able to move on.

Neither choice filled him with any joy.

He was too professional to leave his agent waiting for an answer for too long. If he didn't respond soon, the offer would be rescinded, and some other lucky guy would take his place. Was he a fool for not jumping at the chance? It could well be the only one he'd ever receive. And yet, the money and the fame would only assuage a small part of his heart. Coming to this remote country town on the other side of the world had opened his mind to other possibilities, different challenges and possibly a more fulfilling way of life. All he had to do was decide one way or the other.

And then make a vow never to regret what he'd left behind.

First off – find Billie.

With this goal planted firmly in his mind, he finished

up at the cinema, locking the door behind him when he left. The heat from the setting sun still held sufficient force to hit him like a brick to the face. Instant sweat prickled his skin beneath the light-weight clothes he wore. Taking a sip from the water bottle he carried, he trudged along Mount Ingalls Road which would take him to the gravel road that led to the showgrounds.

Feet were his only transport now. True to her word, Billie had turned up at Fig Tree Lodge the morning after the play and inspected his car. He'd left the keys in the ignition and a note on the windscreen, saying he'd promised to trim the hedges. An offer that had successfully removed him to the rear of the property and well out of sight of Billie. And Sawyer should he accompany her. By the time he'd finished his chore, he had been soaking in sweat and it had been long past mid-day. A piece of paper stuck under a windscreen wiper was the only indication that Billie had ever been there. The result was what he had expected – the engine had blown and unless he wanted to squander a pile of dough there was nothing to be done but have the car towed to the wreckers.

Continuing to move down the road and as his shirt stuck to his clammy back, he wished he'd accepted Dodge and Tessa's offer of a ride. But his lone-wolf act (or sulking as Edwina had termed it at breakfast that morning) was too hard to shake. Instead, he'd mooched along to the cinema, busying himself with a chore that could have waited another week at least. Now he realised he'd been buying time, putting off the moment when he'd come face to face with Billie. Surprisingly, no one living in Fig Tree Lodge had mentioned her name since that fateful night. He'd told no one of the acting offer, and on the surface life had continued much the same as it had previously – apart from the loaded glances and occasional goading comment from Edwina which he had chosen to ignore.

The last burning rays of the sun lit up the heavy clouds in a dazzling display of red and orange, casting a ginger hue over the town. He waved to an old couple who were standing in front of the war memorial ceno-taph in the middle of the intersection, a bunch of wilted flowers intertwined with red and green baubles in their hands which they placed with reverence against the weathered stone. His steps took him past Lette Park where the bore water sprinklers had sprung into action, the swishing sound quite soothing to his jangled soul and where trees that had been planted in another century spread wide branches like offerings to the sky.

It struck him then, as he picked up the pace, striding past the Returned Services League Club before crossing the road how much he liked this town and its inhabitants and how much he wanted to stay. And like a bolt of light-ning, he realised he intended to *'fight'* for Billie.

Even if she could never return his love, she deserved better than someone like Sawyer.

And Kirk was the one to tell her exactly that.

Chapter Thirteen

Bindarra Creek showgrounds often served several different purposes such as a rodeo ring, horse racing and athletics track, circus and country fair area. Tonight, it hosted the annual Carols by Candlelight. On a make-shift stage placed in the centre of the field, the primary school's lower classes stood in their uniforms giving a spirited if slightly off-key version of *Santa Claus is Coming to Town*. Many of the watching adults joined in with gusto and the showground hummed with a magic that only Christmas can generate.

Sitting on the picnic rug with a packed basket ready and waiting, Billie sang at the top of her lungs, relishing the moment. She was alone but with everything she possessed, she hoped that wouldn't be the case for too much longer.

It had taken a good thirty-seven hours to convince Sawyer she wanted nothing more to do with him. At first, his inflated ego couldn't accept the fact and he'd bleated and pleaded running on like an old record until she could have screamed. She'd kept her cool, thanks to the comforting knowledge her parents backed her to the hilt and would have stepped in at any time, should she have asked. Telling Sawyer to never contact her again as well as convincing him he'd never get another dollar out of her, was her problem. But she'd dealt with him and now he was gone – for good.

Then it had taken the rest of the week to muster her courage and make one last bid for Kirk. She'd gone back and forth in her mind about never telling him how she felt and allowing him to disappear to the US without another word from her, to forcing a final encounter where she'd go all out to convince him a life in Bindarra Creek trumped anything else that was on offer. A life with her, of course.

In the end, her need to have him tell her to her face one way or the other won the day – which brought her here to the Carols by Candlelight. A bank of clouds hid the setting sun, deepening the gloom of night far quicker than usual. With the moon hidden, the waving glow sticks in yellows, ambers and green illuminated the grounds, revealing the happy faces of her community. The floodlights near the entrance showed a steady crowd still streaming through the open gates, and people queuing over near a couple of food trucks. No candles were allowed since there was a total fire-ban.

The song came to a wavering conclusion, and everyone applauded. While the kids trooped off the stage and the next act got ready, Billie did another check of the basket's contents; her fav locally made blackberry non-alcoholic wine, a punnet of ripe strawberries from the vicarage garden, a fresh batch of scones, a jar of home-made jam and a carton of cream, kept cold by dint of several freezer blocks snug in a foil-insulated container. She secured the lid once more then twisted round to survey the growing crowd. Next, she checked her mobile. Tessa and Dodge were stationed at the entrance, handing out flyers advertising the benefits of joining either the local volunteer fire brigade or the SES team. Tessa was on look-out duty; the instant she spotted Kirk she was to text Billie. The basket? Well, there was nothing wrong with a bit of food bribery to sweeten the pot. Her parents were somewhere about the grounds, chatting with parishioners and friends, and Billie had paid Eddie, Abby Taylor's youngest boy, to *'house-sit'* Chompers. She was all set for a few hours of zero distractions where she could give her total attention to Kirk.

Her phone buzzed.

HE'S HERE.

. . .

Billie leapt to her feet, heart thrumming like a crazed drummer, to search the sea of people for that one face that had the power to send her senses soaring. Spotting a glimpse of him, she threaded past friends and acquaintances, all of whom seemed to want to chat. With difficulty she prised herself away from the Mayor and his wife who wanted to show her the recent photos they'd received of their grandchild.

And found him.

He stood directly in front of her, his pale lemon tee-shirt and white linen shorts perfectly showcasing his light tan and his intense hazel eyes.

Her breathing seized.

Her eyes all but swallowed him up while the serious expression he wore sent cold trickles along her spine. The lump in her throat grew to gigantic proportions as each waited for the other to speak.

When they did, both spoke at the same time. *"I was hoping to see you." "I'm so glad that you're here."*

Their shared laughter shattered the moment of awkwardness.

"Please, you first," Kirk said.

"I've got a picnic basket," blurted Billie and could have kicked herself. That wasn't what she wanted to say but she was struck with an intense wave of doubt. Instead of confessing her feelings and how much she wanted him to stay, she'd made an inane remark about food. It wasn't even an invitation to share for heaven's sake!

But Kirk seemed to grasp the hidden connotation. "Perfect. Lead on, MacDuff."

The school band launched into a spirited rendition of Jingle Bells as Billie returned to where she'd left the picnic rug and basket, inwardly congratulating herself that she'd chosen a spot surrounded by unfamiliar families. The last thing she wanted tonight was to be sucked into the local gossip or watched by overzealous but well-meaning friends.

She sank onto her knees and turned.

He'd settled onto the cheery green and red blanket a mere breath or two away. So close she could feel the warmth of his body. So close, the temptation to launch herself into his arms mounted with every galloping beat of her runaway heart.

"I've got glow sticks," she said in a feeble attempt to delay that moment when she'd confess it all.

"Perfect."

His gaze never left her face.

Fingers trembling, she fumbled in the basket for a couple of glow sticks, handing one over then cracking hers. "It's a good turn-out. I hope people have been generous with the gold coin donation buckets."

"Billie," he said gruffly, his hand closing over hers where she waved the stupid glow stick distractedly in the air and which she dropped the instant she felt his touch.

This was the moment.

Her last chance.

Tossing all her reservations, her doubts, her insecurities to the four winds, she slipped her hand from his and tenderly cupped the sides of his face. Her eyes straining through the shadows to interpret his expression, she leaned forward and pressed her lips to his.

As a kiss it was short and sweet.

His lips moved beneath hers as he kissed her back. His kiss just as delicate. An affirmation of something stronger than affection. Something powerful that would last all the days of their lives.

They drew back.

Looked at each other.

Smiled.

Suddenly, the need for words, for explanations didn't matter. Not then.

His arms came around her, pressing hard against her back with an urgency that inflamed her passion for this kind and generous man as his mouth claimed hers. Surrendering to the fervour storming through her blood, she matched his hunger with her own. The noise of the crowd, the singing, the laughter, faded into oblivion, a cliché she knew but all she was aware of was Kirk. His heart thumped heavily seemingly in tune with her own as her hands slid down his back and under his shirt. How smooth was his skin as she glided her fingers over his strong muscles, how delicious his lips moving on hers. How much time passed, she wasn't certain when he lifted his head to examine her hot face.

His chest rose and fell rapidly against hers as they both caught their breaths.

"I'm in love with you," he said.

"Ditto."

They grinned. Euphoria gripped Billie, her head giddy with delight as visions of a wonderful future danced in her head. "I'll move to California." The words rushed from her mouth before she even realised she intended to say them.

But he shook his head. "No need, sweetheart. This is where I want to make my home, here in Bindarra Creek with you."

As a declaration it was perfect.

So she rewarded him with another long feverish kiss.

When he drew back, he muttered, "We better stop or we'd better get a room."

"I vote for the room."

He laughed. "So do I but if we're hoping for privacy at Fig Tree Lodge, we'll be out of luck. I'm guessing it won't be any different at your parents' home."

"True," she admitted glumly. "And all the motels are booked out due to Christmas."

Kirk gave her another demanding kiss before saying, "Being with you is enough."

"You say the sweetest things."

"I know." He fluttered his long eyelashes, pretending to be bashful and making her laugh again. "The thing is sweetheart; I don't know if you've noticed but we've got quite an audience."

"Yeah." She grimaced. "I was hoping my parents,

your mum and Auntie Edwina were a figment of my imagination."

"If only." Straightening, but keeping one arm looped around her shoulders, Kirk nodded to their family who had appeared while they had been *'busy'*.

The surrounding people sprawled in camp chairs or on rugs were grinning and when Billie smiled back, several women, including one lady who looked as if she was nearing her hundredth birthday, gave her a thumbs up. Nothing like encouragement.

And nothing like having family share the important moments in life, although she wished they could have waited a bit longer – say a month or two. "Hi Mum, Dad. Everyone."

"Well?" Florrie clasped her hands, looking at them expectantly.

Good question. Billie paused. Not that she needed to reflect for long as Kirk rose to his feet and held out a hand to her father. "Mr Miller, I'd like your permission to marry your daughter."

Jonas peered at Kirk for several seconds. "You like boxing. And baseball. Of course. Nothing would delight me more."

Grinning, Billie jumped up and hugged her parents, then Auntie Edwina who'd remained surprisingly silent albeit she wore a smug smile on her face, and then Louisa.

Her father whispered, "We've got the best Christmas

gift for him. I bought them from Dan yesterday. A pair of boxing gloves."

"Kirk will love it, Dad." Tears sprung to Billie's eyes, although why she would feel like crying at such a perfect moment she didn't know. Perhaps it was knowing that her father had remembered his and Kirk's shared passion for the sports, even if that memory might end up being fleeting. Either way, she'd never forget this night; her family so happy for her, Auntie Edwina acting as if Kirk proposing had all been down to her.

And Kirk.

Kirk gazing at her as if no one and nothing else existed.

Epilogue

"We need to talk."

"Words guaranteed to make even the strongest woman tremble," quipped Billie.

Kirk snickered, planting a kiss on the top of her head.

It was a week later, and they were strolling hand in hand around Lette Park where the community Christmas Eve picnic was well underway. Overhead the sun blazed down with an intensity that made sunnies and hats a must. The park was packed with stalls and people, the noise of the celebrations vibrated in the hot summer air. Excited kids ran here and there, some eating hot dogs or pluto pups, their faces smeared with tomato sauce. Others squealed and hollered in the new water splash pool. Older teenagers queued in straggling lines in front of the giant dart board game and dunking game. There was even a small mob of people waiting outside Auntie Edwina's fortune telling tent.

The mouth-watering scent of barbequed sausages, fried onions and rissoles caused Billie's tummy to rumble even though she'd already had an early morning breakfast down by the river with Kirk and a sausage sandwich when they'd arrived at the park. She couldn't afford to eat any more food. The days before had rolled out in one celebration after another with invitations to dinner, lunches at the Cyprus Café and even a breakfast event hosted by Tessa with the other yoga members in attendance. It seemed that everyone Billie knew wanted to show how pleased they were to hear her special news. If she wanted to fit into her mother's wedding dress even though the event was a good three months distant, then she had to draw the line somewhere. So, no more eating for the day.

Another thirty minutes or so and the fire truck would arrive with Santa. Once he was ensconced on his glittering gold and red throne, the names of all the kids would be read out and each would receive a small gift, courtesy of donations from the local community. It was a tradition that had begun many years ago and which had been dreamt up and organised by the C W A committee.

Meeting Kirk's amused eyes, she murmured, "One of my earliest memories is of this picnic and how excited I was when Santa called out my name and gave me a gift. I couldn't believe he even knew me!" She chuckled.

"You must have been good that year."

"Mmmm, *that* I can't remember. Dad had to walk me up to Santa. I wouldn't go on my own. Oh, wow. Would you believe it? Look! Llamas," she laughed as she spotted Sara and Darim Cooper leading their three animals over to where buckets of water had been placed under a shady tree. She gave them a wave when they looked her way and smiled.

Kirk also lifted his hand and waved vigorously. "You know, I can't believe the number of people I now know. When I first arrived, I knew no one. Barely knew Edwina and her kin. Now – now it feels like I've been a part of this place forever."

"I know what you mean. Mum says there's a kind of magic in Bindarra Creek."

"That I can believe. Because it's where I found you."

She snorted. "Hey. I was the one who found you!"

"Sweetheart – it was all me." He pounded his chest with a fist.

"You are so full of it. But still - I so want to drag you behind that ice cream truck and kiss you - everywhere."

He groaned then sounding as if he was making a monumental effort, dragged in a deep breath and squared his shoulders. "About us and our future. I'm thinking of attending a teacher training college. I've investigated a few places and there's a college in Armidale which isn't too far from here."

"What area would you study?"

"If possible, high school drama. I'd also like to have a go at writing plays for kids. Your thoughts?"

"I think it's a brilliant idea. You'd make a great teacher." She squeezed his fingers.

He attempted to look modest and failed.

Billie rolled her eyes at the tiny smug smile deepening the edges of his lips.

"What can I say? It's a gift I have," he said, repeating back to her the words she'd said to him the night of the play. Eyes glowing with laughter, he tugged her closer.

She leaned in and kissed that smiling mouth. Drawing back, she raised a brow. "What's the catch?"

"I doubt there's much money in it – the play writing I mean, and until I'm qualified, I wouldn't be bringing home much, if any, money." He gave her a worried glance.

"We'll be okay. I've got my casual job at Fred's Garage plus I thought I could set up my own small mechanic shop in Mum and Dad's barn. It's big enough for me to work on one car at a time. Once I've built up a regular clientele, I could look for bigger premises."

"Please don't tell me, we'll be living with them once we're married. I like your parents but not that much." He attempted to look serious, but the gleam of laughter in his eyes was a dead giveaway.

She grinned. "I'll let you off the hook – this time. After Christmas, we'll look for a cottage to rent in town."

"Privacy – at last. I can't wait."

And with that, he swept her into his arms and into a kiss that she knew would last a lifetime.

Thank you so much for purchasing my book, **The Glitter or The Gold**. I hope that you enjoyed discovering how Billie and Kirk forge a new future together, one that is pure gold.

If you enjoyed reading this sweet, small town romance, please recommend this book to your friends. Word of mouth is a wonderful way of discovering new books and authors, and every sale helps me to continue to do what I love – entertaining readers with stories of hope and excitement.

The other books set in this world and written by me which you may also enjoy are (in order of publication): **Bindarra Creek Makeover, Love's Sweet Challenge, Take me Home, A Dangerous Secret** and **The Mistletoe Wish**.

Until next time.

About the Multi-Author Bindarra Creek Romance Series

Welcome to Bindarra Creek, a struggling country town where people work hard and love deeply. Set in the picturesque tablelands of New England, Australia, Bindarra Creek is a fictional, rural community full of romance, intrigue, adventure, drama and suspense.

This latest series, **Bindarra Creek Small Town Christmas**, is the sixth multi-best-selling author 'series' set in the fictional small town of Bindarra Creek.

Bindarra Creek Small Town Christmas – released 1st December 2023

The Glitter or The Gold – Suzanne Gilchrist (aka S E Gilchrist)

Christmas at the Cyprus Café – Susanne Bellamy

A Place to Belong – Annie Seaton

A Magical Summer - Rhonda Forrest

Destined to Stay – Kerrie Paterson
Home for Christmas – Lauren K McKellar
The Christmas Surprise – Linda Charles
The Gift of Bindarra Creek – Lindsay Douglas

The other series are as follows:

A Bindarra Creek Christmas Romance - 2022
The Mistletoe Wish – Suzanne Gilchrist (aka S E Gilchrist)
The Christmas Jinx – Susanne Bellamy
The Grinch of Bindarra Creek – Lindsay Douglas
Christmas at Forrest Glen - Rhonda Forrest
Mistletoe Magic – Erin Moira O'Hara
Mistletoe and Blue Jeans – Linda Charles
A Clever Christmas – Annie Seaton
Tangled by Tinsel – Phillipa Nefri Clark
A Cowboy for Christmas – Lauren K McKellar

A Bindarra Creek Mystery Romance - 2022
A Dangerous Secret – Suzanne Gilchrist (aka S E Gilchrist)
Beyond the Gate – Rhonda Forrest
Protecting their Destiny – Erin Moira O'Hara
Only She Knew – Linda Charles
Secrets of River Cottage – Annie Seaton
Forgotten Secrets – Susanne Bellamy
A Perfect Danger – Phillipa Nefri Clark

Bindarra Creek A Town Reborn

Take Me Home – Suzanne Gilchrist (aka S E Gilchrist)

In the Heat of the Night – Susanne Bellamy

No Looking Back - Linda Charles

Worth the Wait – Annie Seaton

With Every Breath – Lauren K. McKellar

Stealing Her Heart – Simone Angela

A Twist of Fate – Erin Moira O'Hara

Promise Me Forever – Juanita Kees

Bindarra Creek Short & Sweet

What's in a Kiss - Linda Charles

My Forever Valentine – Sandie James (not available)

Pearls and Green Beer – Susanne Bellamy

Full Circle – Annie Seaton

Date with Destiny – Erin Moira O'Hara

A Letter From the Queen – Lee Christine

Love's Sweet Challenge – Suzanne Gilchrist (aka S E Gilchrist)

The Widow Maker – Lauren K. McKellar

Out of the Blue – Noelle Clark

Bindarra Creek Romance

Bindarra Creek Makeover - S E Gilchrist

Shadows of the Heart - Lee Christine

Second Chance Love - Susanne Bellamy

The CEO Mechanic - Sandie James (not available)

Reach for the Stars - Kerrie Paterson

Home to Bindarra Creek - Juanita Kees

Stolen Sanctuary - Stacey Nash
Tempting Fate - Erin Moira O'Hara
One More Day - Linda Charles
The Vine - Lauren K. McKellar
The Ghost of His Past - Simone Angela
Joanie's Dilemma - Marianne Theresa
Buckley's Chance - Noelle Clark

All books are available as ebooks, some are available also as paperbacks.

Every book can be read as a stand alone, however reading the series as a whole will give you more insight into our fictional community as the town continues to grow and change. There is drama, suspense, mystery and just simply feel-good clean and wholesome romance.

For more info on Bindarra Creek Romances, visit www.bindarracreekromance.com

Acknowledgments

My special thanks go to the following wonderful women:

Cindy Pearson for her awesome proof-reading skills;

and

Ann B Harrison and Erin Moira O'Hara for giving up
their time to critique my manuscript.

To the other authors in the *Bindarra Creek Small Town
Christmas* series – it's been a pleasure working with you.

In the spirit of reconciliation, the author and publisher
acknowledges Aboriginal and Torres Strait Islander
peoples as the First Australians and Traditional
Custodians of the lands where we live, learn and work.
We pay our respects to Elders past and present and all
First Nations peoples and honour their unique cultural
and spiritual relationships to the land, waters and seas

and their rich contribution to society, and for their ongoing custodianship of and care for Country.